I0661666

Samuel Crothers Logan

The Life of Thomas Dixon

A Memorial

Samuel Crothers Logan

The Life of Thomas Dixon
A Memorial

ISBN/EAN: 9783337414726

Printed in Europe, USA, Canada, Australia, Japan

Cover: Foto ©Raphael Reischuk / pixelio.de

More available books at **www.hansebooks.com**

THE LIFE

OF

THOMAS DICKSON.

𝕬 𝕸𝖊𝖒𝖔𝖗𝖎𝖆𝖑.

BY

SAMUEL C. LOGAN, D.D.

SCRANTON, PA., 1888.

To

Sophia Dickson Torrey,

Elizabeth Dickson Boies, James Pringle Dickson,

Joseph Benjamin Dickson,

And their Children,

IS THIS IMPERFECT MEMORIAL OF THEIR VENERATED FATHER

AFFECTIONATELY DEDICATED BY

The Author,

WHO THROUGH MANY YEARS OF PERSONAL AND PASTORAL

ASSOCIATION COUNTED IT ONE OF HIS CHOICE PRIVILEGES

TO BE RECOGNIZED AS ONE OF THIS WORTHY

FATHER'S PERSONAL FRIENDS.

THIS, TOO,

WITH THE SPECIAL DESIRE THAT THE COVENANT BLESSING

THAT THOMAS DICKSON INHERITED FROM HIS

PIOUS ANCESTRY, MAY,

WITH HIS MANY MANLY AND CHRISTIAN VIRTUES, DESCEND

TO THEM, AND TO THEIR CHILDREN, TO THE

REMOTEST GENERATION.

CONTENTS.

The Memorial.

§

ITS OBJECTS AND LIMITATIONS.

I HAVE been requested to write a memorial of my departed friend, Mr. Thomas Dickson, which shall be especially intended for the use of his family and immediate friends. This work I cheerfully undertake, both out of interest in the living and of love for the dead. Mr. Dickson's long identification with the great schemes of industry in the Lackawanna Valley, and his high character as a citizen, would seem to demand that his life should not be permitted to pass away from the memory of the world without some monument commemorative of his work and his excellence. When future historians shall seek to trace the history of the industries and record the wonderful development of society in the growing communities of north-eastern Pennsylvania, no doubt some permanent general record will show the connection of Mr. Dickson's life and labors with this development; and it is well that material should be provided by which such history may be made truthful and just.

It is perhaps impossible for one generation fully to apprehend the life, or appreciate the experiences, of the generation which precedes it. It is chiefly the issues of an active life, with its accomplished facts which touch other lives in this world, which may be expected to make lasting impressions on succeeding generations. A man's contemporaries are the most capable and appreciative judges of his personal character; while an after-generation may perhaps be the better judge of his acts, or of the wisdom of his plans. IT IS THE MEMORY OF THE MAN, not the register of his deeds, which is the more precious to his friends. The deeds are to them specially valuable only in so far as they perpetuate the picture of the man himself. It is the husband, the father, and friend, who should be embalmed in the deserted household and circle of affection. His works and activities will be measured by them, and become especially precious only in so far as they bring the man himself back in his earnest and active life to their hearts.

It is, indeed, one of the saddest thoughts of our lives here, that we not only pass away from visible and conscious contact with the world, which is so much to us, but that the very remembrance of us fades away from the world's vision, as the morning cloud before the dawning of the day. The remembrance of many of our acts and plans of life may remain in the world after we leave it, especially if their results continue to affect other lives. Dim and imperfect shadows of ourselves, in conspicuous positions, may now and then flash across the path of other seekers of position ; we shall probably be lost to sight, even before the foot-prints we have made, in crossing the stage of action, have become untraceable. Yet it is we ourselves who desire to live in the hearts of all to whom we have tried to be helpful and true. It is what we are, or have tried to be, with all our mistakes and blunders, our imperfections and weaknesses, that we desire should remain in the memory and heart of those we leave behind us.

There are perhaps three separate forces which, more than all others, combine to determine the lives of such men as Thomas Dickson in this world. The influences of each of these forces must be considered . in any true biography. The first of these is that which the Christian must recognize as the work of God, manifested in the individual characteristics of the soul. There is such a thing as a patent of personal origin, which must be carried with us through

all life.   There are gifts and endowments which
mark our personality in the great family of God —
characteristics determined directly by the Creator of
the individual.   The second force is that of one's
parentage, in which are to be traced the mysterious
power of blood and the effective forces of the earthly
origin.   The third of these forces are the circumstances of life, especially in its formative stages, and
in the junctures which bring out and direct its latent
forces.   There is a double relationship of the individual, which will be found to be forceful throughout
life.   This relationship is to one's experiences, and
circumstances; by which human action, thought, and
feeling are so frequently determined.   But above
and beyond all these we shall discover in every man
who makes a position for himself a distinct personality — a native manhood, which he has received
directly from his Maker.   In this memorial it is proposed to keep in view and preserve in their proportions these controlling influences as they are seen
to crystallize in the beauty, harmony, and force of a
useful life.

The record which is here proposed is simply that
of a few of the way-marks of an active and useful life
of three-score years, to the end of giving the man
himself his true place in the memory of his children.
So far as it is a record of facts, it will be that of a
few of the incidents and struggles in a life which was
conspicuous for its industry and its peacefulness; for

its success and sunshine; for its public force and its private virtues. It was a life of more than ordinary excellence in public trusts; of more than common consistency in private virtue, in all its relationships and responsibilities. Merely a condensed statement of facts, it must be, which are yet well known to his friends and associates.

The proper record of a busy life, of even half a century, can only be fully written by him whose "book of remembrance" is closed to this world.

Much less may we attempt to trace the sweep or measure the fruits of such a life, with their continually acting power. We may perpetuate for a time the way-marks of an earthly pilgrimage, and note some of the "foot-prints left on the sands of time" before they are forever effaced, and so gather lessons for our life and blessing. This is all that is here proposed. A simple household memorial of a richly endowed and faithful father, who lived for his family, under an acknowledged stewardship from God. A memorial by which, though dead, he shall continue to speak to those that remain and to those yet to come. A family tablet it is to be; set up in the deserted home, to perpetuate benedictions of wisdom and love to all the households through which his blood shall continue to flow. THAT TABLET READS AS FOLLOWS:

I.

NATIVITY, PARENTAGE, MIGRATION, EARLY RESPONSIBILITIES.

THOMAS DICKSON was born March the 26th,
A. D. eighteen hundred and twenty-four, at
the town of Leeds, in England, during a temporary
residence of his parents in that place. The family
home was at Lauder, in Berwickshire, Scotland. But
for a time, for the purpose of his industry, Mr.
Dickson's father had taken his family to Leeds,
without intention of permanent residence, and a
short time after the birth of Thomas the family returned to Lauder. Hence Thomas always reckoned
himself a Scotchman, both geographically and by
blood. He defended his birthright by asserting that
if he had been born in a sty it would not make him

a pig; or, if he had arrived in the world beside a mill-pond, and had learned to swim before he migrated, it could hardly make him a goose. He was the first-born child of James Dickson, a millwright of Lauder, and of Elizabeth Linen, who was a native of the same region. He was a scion of one of those Presbyterian families which laid the broad foundations of the Scottish civilization and greatness. He inherited a name and a blood which is traceable backward through many generations, and which comes to the surface with conspicuous distinctness in the special times of exigency and of heroic sacrifice for the right, in Scottish history.

The grandfather of Thomas Dickson, whose name he inherited, served his country for twenty years as a member of the 92d Regiment of Highlanders. This man married at the age of fifteen, and was a father at the age of sixteen. This youthful father enlisted as a boy, and served heroically in his regiment throughout the stormy times of the Napoleonic conquests.

For twenty years he marched, fought, and suffered with his regiment for his country. He went through the Peninsular campaign, when the French, under Jerome Bonaparte, were driven out of Spain. He stood immovable in the shock of that last charge of the French at Waterloo, where Scotch persistency became the anchorage of British glory. This Thomas Dickson was one of the three men of his company

who were found standing, full armed, when that
charge ended and Napoleon's sun set forever. He
received from the British Government conspicuous
medals and military decorations for his valor, upon
which were inscribed the names of fifty-two battles
in which he so valiantly fought. These mementos
of heroic services were inherited by his son James,
who was only sixteen years younger than himself,
and who was Thomas Dickson's father. They are
still in the possession of the family, an heirloom of
which any family may be proud.

James Dickson, the son of the soldier, and the
worthy millwright of Lauder, was trained by his
young mother, and was a man of decided religious
convictions. He, with his excellent wife, early identified himself with the Presbyterian Church, of which,
during the latter half of his life, he was an efficient
ruling elder. He was a man of great patience and
industry, of carefulness and simple tastes. When
old age compelled his retirement from business, he
spent much of his time in writing short sermons,
modeled after the general style of the Scottish
divines. With these discourses he entertained his
friends and family, and made them useful in the absence of his pastor in the social meetings of the
church.

In the year 1832 James Dickson made up his
mind to try his fortunes in the New World. Breaking
the ties which bound his family to their native

heather, he embarked, in company with his wife's
brother, John Linen, who was a successful artist, in a
sailing vessel from the port of Glasgow. These
men sailed from Scotland with little expectation of
ever being permitted to return. They took with
them their families and all their effects. Dickson
and his wife were blessed with six healthy children,
of whom Thomas was the oldest, then a lad of nine
years. They were more than nine weeks tossing
through a stormy passage, driven by adverse winds.
The perils and discomforts of this voyage made a
permanent impression upon the mind of the young
lad Thomas. In the later years of his life he was
accustomed to tell the story of the family migration
with a pathos which touched the heart and drew tears
from the eyes of his auditors. For more than two
months they were tossed, and suffered, on the bois-
terous ocean, and at the end of that time they anchored in the mouth of the St. Lawrence. Here the
families were transferred to bateaux, with a whole
company of emigrants, in which they were towed up
the current of the great river by oxen walking on
the banks. In this voyage of the migration the
boy Thomas learned a lesson of patience, perseverance, and endurance under difficulties, which fitted
him for the experiences of a pioneer life, which he
was so early to encounter. The sorrows of this
voyage up the St. Lawrence were greatly increased
by an attack upon Thomas of the cholera, which for

the first time appeared in America in that summer of 1832.

James Dickson stopped with his family at Toronto, and attempted to follow the business of his trade. But the country was so new, the settlements so sparse, and the machinery so rude and imperfect, that there was little prospect of either brilliant or permanent success. He struggled hard to get a foot-hold, but grew discouraged with the prospect; and at length, in 1834, followed his friend and relative, George Linen, who had migrated the year following that of his brother, to Dundaff, which was a new settlement at the foot of Elk Mountain, in north-eastern Pennsylvania. Here Mr. Dickson placed his family on a farm, where the two friends very soon demonstrated that the artist and millwright were but poor material to convert into farmers. Early discovering that he could not hope to be a successful farmer, Mr. Dickson abruptly left the whole farm venture in the care of his young son Thomas and his mother, while he ventured to New-York in search for employment as a mechanic. Here he found work which speedily developed into a hopeful opening, by reason of the unusual demand for the work of mechanics which was consequent upon the great fire of 1835. Here James Dickson spent two winters, with their intervening summer, in successful work; at the end of which time he returned to Dundaff, with the intention of taking his family with him to settle in the city. But while he tarried with his family in the visitation of his old friends at Carbondale, he became acquainted with the president and other officers of the Delaware and Hudson Canal Company.

This company had been organized in 1824 — the year of Thomas Dickson's birth — in the city of New-York. It was organized especially for the mining and transportation of coal, with its offices in the city of New-York, while the point of its operations was at and about Carbondale, in the Lackawanna Valley. Up to the time of Mr. Dickson's acquaintance with it, all the machinery of this company, except that which lifted cars up the planes upon a horse-railway, had been operated by water-power, and it labored under all the difficulties of the undeveloped coal enterprise of that day.

The attention of the president of this company was called to Mr. Dickson, because of his being a skilled millwright, with his family already in the field of operations. As soon as his skill was known, Mr. Dickson was offered the position of mechanic among the water-wheels and in the rude shops of the company. Hence in the spring of 1836 he accepted employment in this capacity, and moved his family from Dundaff to Carbondale. Here he entered permanently the service of the Delaware and Hudson Canal Company, and by his skill and sound judgment he soon won the position of master mechanic. This position he held with honor, and prosecuted its enlarging work with decided success. And even when old age had set him aside from active duty, he was retained in his honorable position until the year of his death, in 1880. In this worthy position, James Dickson was permitted to support his family and educate his successful sons and daughters. Throughout his life he illustrated, in the community, the excellencies of a consistent Christian character.

James Dickson's wife, Elizabeth Linen, was the master-spirit and formative power in the household. She was a woman of more than ordinary natural endowments, which prepared her for every exigency. The family after their migration were subjected to great trials and reduced to a very narrow margin in daily life. But Mrs. Dickson, burdened with the care of her six small children, never lost heart, hope, or patience. She took charge of the whole household, after the style of the "guid Scotch wife." Her husband regularly intrusted her with his wages, and she applied them with great wisdom for the support of the family. James Dickson fully appreciated his wife, and was as one of his own children in all matters of the household. His wife purchased for him his clothes, as she did that of her children, and directed his holidays' expenditures, what few he had. She, by her genius and spirit, ordered the household so that it was full of love and cheerfulness, with all its burdens and anxieties. With persevering economy and endless labor, she clothed her family, so that her children might lift up their heads with the best of the community. Crowded in the little cabin, she might have been seen, almost any night, with an umbrella spread over her to hide the light from the eyes of her sleeping husband and children, while she cut and patched and altered the garments of her children, asleep all about her. To the best natural gifts this woman added the most lovely Christian spirit, and was possessed of the best education of the times. She lived to see her sons and daughters more than ordinarily successful in life, and died leaving a whole community to mourn her departure and to remember her virtues.

During the hard winter which succeeded James Dickson's departure to New-York from Dundaff, the farm he had rented was left, as has been said, in the care of Thomas and his mother; and during this winter Thomas developed many characteristics which followed him through life—characteristics which enabled him to make friends of all classes of men. He used, after he had reached his great success in business, to tell of his schemes and trials when snowed in among the hills of Dundaff with his beloved mother and her family of bairns, as he was accustomed to call them, with small supplies and none to help them. With the vivacity and sparkle that always filled his auditors with laughter, he gave descriptions and accounts of his experiences and suf-

ferings, which made, as he said, the winter full twelve
months long.   His greatest difficulty was to find
suitable wood in that dense forest to keep the cabin
warm enough to avoid freezing.   The snow had a
power of penetration which, he said, would hunt out
the baby through every crack.   He said that he and
his mother at least "were kept in a sweat all winter."

The pictures he drew of himself clothed in the
garments which his father had left behind him, and
which his mother persuaded him he would speedily
fill with a full-rounded manhood, were unique. With
pantaloons drawn up to his armpits, and rolled up
at the bottom to keep them from entangling his feet,
and a coat whose skirts were more dangerous than
the legs of the pants he wore, he toiled day after day,
with a yoke of oxen to snake the logs from the forest
for fire-wood.   With all his industry and perseverance he found that his work was only fairly begun
when he had brought the logs to the cabin door.
He was consequently led to conclude that a successful worker must be one who can set others to work,
and legitimately use their more abundance of power
to supplement his own energies.   He concluded that
he had better use his wits as well as his muscle, or
else he might awake some morning to find his precious charge frozen stiff.   Hence he went to an old
merchant of Dundaff, Charles Welles by name, and
told the story of his trials, his perplexities and fail-
ures, and asked for a loan of a few dollars to help

him "out of the woods." The old merchant became interested in the spirit and story of the boy, and furnished him with excellent advice as well as the funds to help him secure wood-choppers to prepare the wood for the family's use. Thomas, instead of attempting to hire wood-choppers, spent all his money for the best Scotch whisky, and invited the whole neighborhood to a chopping-bee. The neighbors gathered from far and near, and in one day this boy of less than twelve years solved the almost hopeless problem, and provided the household with an excellent supply of winter fuel. This, his first venture in business, gave him a key to the stewardship of a successful business life. To bind his fellows to himself and to his schemes of industry, by genial fellowship and good cheer, became the plan of his working; and no man ever carried out greater plans of industry with more real satisfaction to those who became identified with him, or were employed as his willing helpers.

II.

EDUCATION AND .EDUCATORS — LITERARY TASTES AND PURSUITS.

OF the education of Thomas Dickson, technically speaking, very little can be said. He was not what we should be willing to call "a self-made man," as that phrase is usually employed. He was too good and great to be placed for a moment in that class of men whose usual boast is that they are "self-made." We should much prefer to call him a home-made man of the very best style. He was the product of a worthy Christian household and of a parental training of the best order.

It would be very difficult for his children, and certainly impossible for his grandchildren, to reach any adequate conception of the conditions of the pio-

neer life to which his childhood and youth were subjected. It would be difficult, if not impossible, for
this generation to form a true measurement of what
are generally called the educational privileges under
which he pressed his way to manhood and marked
out the path of his life.

The pioneers who hewed down the forests, and laid
the foundations of a country that in a single generation has leaped to the front in the march of a world's
civilization, almost without exception, were believers
in the power and necessity of Christian education, as
the efficient factor of a free people. Their first
work, after the establishing of their own rude homes
in the wilderness, was the building of the school-
house and the house of worship. But the means at
their command and the conveniences within their
reach were so limited, that it was generally at the
sacrifice of the educational interests of the first generation that respectable schools were established in
any community.

Teachers who were really qualified to conduct a
school were very few, and hard to obtain; while the
compensation of such teachers was so meager that
they were compelled to spend the summer months in
other business, so as to gather a sufficient living to
enable them to teach through the winter. The
school-teachers of the first third of the present century, especially outside of New England, were mostly
Protestant Irishmen. They were men whose chief

2

ideas of training young minds revolved about a narrow theory of strict discipline, and the various relations of "superiors, inferiors, and equals," as suggested by the Heidelberg or Westminster Catechisms. The common school was a little kingdom, of which the teacher was the king; and his chief work was that of government. Unless the boys and girls were taken up by the pastor, as a work of love and Christian duty, their education must be limited to the merest rudiments of what was called an English education. The books and appliances for the convenience of teachers were as angular and inferior, in general, as were the teachers themselves.

A sketch of the school in actual session will, perhaps, give us a clearer estimate of the value of school privileges, as they were enjoyed by the boys of the generation to which Mr. Dickson belonged. Here it is. Suppose a log-cabin twenty by thirty feet, with one log cut out for the greater part of its length, on the side opposite to the door. The vacancy thus made was closed to the weather, first by greased paper, and then, as the arts of life advanced, by single panes of glass, set up side by side, to admit the light. This was the window of the school-house. A long board, resting upon pins driven into the wall at an angle of forty-five degrees, formed a writing-desk; and a slab, perched upon legs three feet long, which forbade the possibility of the urchins' feet touching the floor, constituted the preparations for learning to write. Upon this long bench the chickens of the community, great and small, were perched, and learned to use the quill of the goose. The work of the first winter was generally confined to the mere scratching of what were called "pot-hooks," or imitations of the curves of the iron hooks hanging upon the cranes of their mothers' kitchens. A box stove, with an open oven, which was chiefly convenient for the roasting of apples, occupied the center of the room. This luxurious heater was usually filled with green wood, from the forest, that could only with persistent coaxing be induced to burn, and had its smoke-pipe running out through the roof in such a way as to be dependent upon the wind to determine whether the smoke should pass up or down. An elevated desk, or throne, for the use of the teacher, was placed at the end of the room, and slabs on short legs filled the remainder of the floor. Here sat the pupils in long rows, graded according to degrees of progress, social status, or length of limbs ; but generally all seated so high as to be allowed full room for the swinging of their feet, by which they kept time with their puzzled thoughts, and rendered tolerable, by constant exercise, the sedentary life to which they were compelled. The first and second rows of these urchins flourish in their hands, or hold before their faces, shingles which are carved into paddles of various patterns, on one side of which are the letters of the alphabet, and the combination of these letters in square onion-beds of "a-b abs"; on the other the mysteries of mathematics which are crystallized in the multiplication-table, and in the various tables of *measure*, both "liquid" and "dry." These were their books, or literary works, containing the rudiments of knowledge, and were usually provided by the pen of the teacher. Next to these sat the row of those in the second class, holding well-thumbed spelling-books, which were the contribution to the world's life and advancement made by Dillworth and Webster. Next to these the reading-classes, who are poring over appointed tasks in the "English Reader," which is a book made up of extracts from the works of the English masters in prose and poetry. Along with these are reading-classes in the Old and New Testaments. These constitute all the reading-books known to the community which may be useful to the school. "Pike's Arithmetic," with its teaching all shackled with "pounds, shillings, and pence," with the treatise on prosody which they called "grammar," which was relegated to the appendix of the spelling-book, constitute the sum of the helps for the highest education proposed.

Such was the school of 1830 among the mountains and in the valley about Carbondale. A higher education than could be afforded by such a school could be found only at great expense or else through the self-denial of ministers and missionaries who selected special pupils for private and classic tuition, and at their own cost usually prepared them for college.

When the Dickson family were safely housed in their home of two rooms and a kitchen in Carbondale, and the father had found steady work among the water-wheels and lifting-sweeps of the Delaware and Hudson Canal Company, it was at once decided that Thomas should take up the broken threads of his education, which hitherto had been running entirely between himself and his beloved mother. She was more proud of her boy and of his capabilities than she was of his advancement in book knowledge. She had done the best she could for him in her teaching, but she earnestly coveted for him a generous education. It was therefore determined to place him in the village school. It was the best the town could afford for the boys. It was taught by an Irishman by the name of John Welch. A regular knight of the rod he was, perpetually burdened with the cares of government, in his little commonwealth.

There were two characteristics of the boy Thomas which were inwoven with the texture of his being — characteristics which could be neither eliminated nor hidden throughout a long life. The first of these was an innate love of fun, absolutely irrepressible; the other a love of justice, honesty, and fair dealing under all circumstances. These peculiarities were

as strong in the child as they ever were in the man,
and they carried a beautiful array of virtues along
with them in all his life.   For the enjoyment of his
fun he was ready to turn the house upside down at
any time.   He was always ready to get his fellows
into all kinds of difficulties ; but then he stepped up
like a man, and either laughed the government out
of its judicial severity, or took the punishment due for
transgression for the whole lot, if need required,
without flinching.   By his own confession he usually
paid the score of all the poor sinners whom he
had inveigled into transgression.   Thomas asserted
through after life, in his joking way, that he had
taken the chastisement for all his brothers and sisters
as a household duty, and had thus been the means
of their best education.   But all dishonest shirking
and falsehood he abhorred.   He was neither guilty
of it himself nor would he ever suffer it in others, if
he could help it.   These two peculiarities were the
means of cutting short his education in the Irish
academy of the executive Welch.   He had been in
school but a few weeks, exploring the mysteries of
"Pike's Arithmetic," when he came into collision most
unexpectedly with the powers that were.   It was
after this manner.   The pupils were gathered about
the stove, with its enormous burden of green wood,
each trying to extract enough of heat to satisfy his
toes, or at least melt the snow from his shoes, when
a boy at the end of the row, led by the spirit of mis-

chief which was well known to dwell in the Scotch lad, brought his weight suddenly against this row of small "bricks," just for the fun of seeing them tumble over each other, and so demonstrate the law of the resistance of solids and the accurate relations of force and momentum.

Thomas was immediately called to the teacher's bar of justice and charged with this crime, of which he was himself one of the victims. He was ordered to hold out his hand for punishment for this disorderly conduct. Thomas denied the charge with a hot indignation, which was greatly increased by the fact that the real culprit was a favorite of the teacher, and one who, by his silence, proposed to allow the innocent to suffer. He refused to submit to the unjust discipline, and immediately showed the teacher a clean pair of heels. Around and around the stove and over the benches ran the fugitive from justice, with the wand of punishment flourishing behind him in the hand of the irate master. Thomas discovered that the tongs have entire advantage over the compasses by their length of limb, and hence that the master was gaining upon the culprit as the race continued. But as he passed the teacher's desk he snatched up his inkstand and hurled it with precision, and telling force, at the teacher's head, and then shot out of the school-house door. Thus he graduated, or at least completed the assigned curriculum of his school education.

He went home immediately and reported the whole state of the case to his father, who advised him to return and apologize for his rebellion to his teacher, and take his punishment like a man. This he refused absolutely to do, upon the assertion that it was a demand to submit to an injustice, which he never could consent to endure. His father then hastily told him if he could not reconcile himself to his teacher he must go to work. He accepted the alternative with unexpected promptness, and set out to find a job, at once determined to start upon the highway of life for himself. He applied to one George A. Whiting for a position, expressing his willingness to try his hand at anything. Mr. Whiting was connected with the coal-works of the Delaware and Hudson Canal Company, and at once became interested in the spirit and energy of the boy. He gave him the job of driving the very large mule harnessed at the sweep, and used for lifting coal out of the mine. The superintendent furnished him with this large, headstrong beast, and told him to go and try his hand. The little fellow mounted the animal's back to ride him down to the sweep, where his daily task was appointed, but the mule rebelled; and after various gyrations going about half-way to the sweep, having, perhaps, carefully considered the weight of the governing power having hold of the reins, he turned himself about and brought the boy back to the store; much to his own chagrin, and to the

amusement of the men and boys who had gathered
to see the contest at the entrance of the young man
on the business of life. But by persistence and pluck
Thomas succeeded in mastering the unruly force
which was put under his charge, and brought his
living engine to a faithful duty at the mines. Here
he began his business life, which was ultimately to
win for him his high position.

From the time young Dickson so rashly left the
school his education was chiefly in his own hands.
It was in no sense the result of his want of interest
in books, or of an appreciation of the best school
education, that he had turned his back upon the
village school. Doubtless a respectable compromise
could have been secured with this teacher who had
outraged his sense of justice, and the popularity of
the lad in the community would have given him the
best position in the school itself. It was rather due
to the awakening of the young manhood in him,
which suggested independent action for his own self-
support.

From childhood he had manifested a taste for
study and a longing for books. He had read everything his parents possessed; but the desire to work
his own way, or "to paddle his own canoe," as he
expressed it, and to relieve his overtaxed parents of
any further care either for his support or education,
led him to accept at once his father's offer of the
alternative that if he would not return to school

he should go to work. This proposal of his father was doubtless made without thought of the possibility of his accepting it, and with the expectation that he would go back to school. But the alternative of school, with submission to a teacher for whom he had lost respect, or work and wages under his own control, however hard the one or limited the other, to such a boy as he was, brought the issue and decision which no one who knew him in after life could have failed to expect.

We are not to suppose that Thomas threw away all privileges of education when he harnessed himself to the mine-sweep with its unruly beast, to become "a mule-driver at the mines," and so set up for himself. He was born with a love of books, and read everything within his reach. After he had settled himself as salesman in a store of promiscuous merchandise, one Silas S. Benedict came to Carbondale, and proved himself an excellent teacher. He greatly quickened the interest of the young people in books and in the search for knowledge; and Thomas for a time placed himself under this teacher's private tuition. Here he made rapid advancement, and remained long enough to become a leader in the public exhibitions of the young people of the village, by which Mr. Benedict stimulated the progress of his pupils in literary composition, in declamation, and in public debate. Here Thomas gained his first laurels in a literary way.

At this period a scheme for the education of young men became general in the country in the way of literary societies and debating clubs. By these village and neighborhood societies many a young man, on the frontier, prepared himself for usefulness and success in public life. It was in such a club that Abraham Lincoln found one of his great educators. Young Dickson became one of the leaders that organized such a society in Carbondale, and in it he found great help toward the development of his mental resources. Once a week the young men gathered together, declaimed speeches, read essays, and debated the questions of public interest of all sorts. Occasionally the doors of the club were thrown open to the public for the double purpose of testing the mettle of the performers and of cultivating the good-will of the people. With these literary societies were often connected public spelling-matches and reading associations, when the people gathered to witness the progress, and enjoy the promiscuous contests, of the young people in their efforts to educate themselves. Then, for the education and exercise of the social life of the young people, singing-schools were appointed and encouraged, which opened a free field for the conquest of hearts, and for the tuning of the young gentlemen and young ladies for the march of life together. It was in these literary and social associations that Thomas Dickson laid the broad foundations for the successful and use-

ful life which he lived, and for the holding of his
leading position among his fellows.

The effect of this training was evident in the interest which he in all his life manifested in books and
libraries. As soon as, in the advancement of his life,
he had entered into business with Mr. Benjamin as a
partner in that promiscuous store, which included
both an iron foundry and a drug department, this
young man, at his own expense, gathered books to
form a circulating library. These books he placed
in his drug store, and for a small fee he loaned them
to be read and returned. The fees for the reading
were applied to the payment for the books, and then
to the purchase of new books as the plan succeeded.
This library he kept in Carbondale as long as he
was in business there, and it proved a benefaction
to the whole settlement. Thus his interest in the
advancement and well-being of the people began
very early in life, and it continued without abate-
ment throughout his career. Along with the good
accomplished among his associates, male and female,
by cultivating in them a taste for reading, and so
manifestly in lifting up society in a new settlement,
it must not be forgotten that he secured direct advantage to himself. Pushed out in life with no more
education than his hard-working father and over-
worked mother could give him, his thirst for that
knowledge which could only be found in books, was
awakened, in good measure, by the position of lead-

ership in the young society to which his popular
characteristics pushed him.

He seemed to possess an innate love of poetry, and
very early became familiar with the Scottish bards,
whose songs he had learned from his mother and
which he carried with him through life. He was
equally captivated by the heroic in the history of his
native land.   Hence, by the enterprise of his circulating library, by which he proposed to make the
readers pay for the books by small installments, he
increased his own store of knowledge, and thus became a rapid and careful reader.   In time he became
a sort of extemporaneous encyclopedia of such poets
as Ramsay, Tom Moore, and Burns, as well as of
the masterly stories of Scott, the letters of Addison,
and essays of Charles Lamb.   His love of declamation led him from these to the pages of Shakspere,
until, as he often told me, his love of books had been
a snare to him all his life.   He had to resist this love
of reading to prevent its interference with his duties
in business trusts and responsibilities.   He often said
to his friends, after he had passed the meridian of his
life, that he believed he ought to have been a literary
man ; and he never ceased to express his regret
that he had been denied the privilege of a classic
education.

Soon after he removed from Carbondale, leaving
his circulating library, and had come to Scranton to
enter upon his great business enterprise, he began

systematically to collect books for a library for himself and his family. Keeping a strict account of his income and expenses, he systematically devoted a certain amount yearly to the purchase of books, and tried to read them as fast as he was able to place them in his library. In this work he succeeded until his prosperity and his enlarged business responsibilities both gave him a greater number of books than he could possibly master, and allowed him less time to read them. For many years he "limited himself," as he called it, to the expenditure of $500 a year for the purchase of new books. He was accustomed to excuse himself to his cheerful wife for what might seem to her an extravagance in this direction, by saying that as he neither spent money for drink nor beastly pleasure, he thought she ought to allow him this decent folly; which, of course, she was always too happy to do. His collection of books, of the first order, continued as long as he lived. In time he built a beautiful room for these books, which opened from the family sitting-room in his homestead in Scranton, and filled it with the choicest works in the English language, on all subjects. Gradually this library overflowed until the family room had all its vacant spaces around the walls occupied with standard works. A few years before his death Mr. Dickson had his library conveniently catalogued, and left more than six thousand volumes to his estate worthy of a place in any library. It was generally believed to be the best private library within the State of Pennsylvania, and he enjoyed and used its treasures as long as he lived.

His literary efforts, in a limited way, began quite early. Among the associates of his youth Thomas Dickson frequently appeared before a limited public in addresses upon occasion of public celebrations, and especially before benevolent associations, of which he early became the master-spirit. He took special interest in the organization of these benevolent societies, both because of their charitable and social benefits among the young men of the community. He was particularly interested in the Caledonian societies, and, as long as he lived, took part in the celebration of the natal day of their favorite poet, Robert Burns.

His speeches on these occasions were received with great gratification, due in some measure, perhaps, to his individual popularity, but more especially because they were generally spiced with his sparkling vivacity and fun, which bubbled up and ran in a perpetual overflow from the exuberance of his daily life. In his contact with the world and associations in life, to tease and perpetrate practical jokes upon all whom he liked seemed to give zest to his very existence; and this disposition continued with him under all vicissitudes. As long as he lived his buoyancy of spirit never failed him. His sparkling wit and quiet humor were as constant as his daily bread.

In his social intercourse with all classes he always found it necessary to have some one to tease, whether in his office, in the shop, or at his home.

His love of letters, and especially of poetry, was illustrated by a habit which his wife testifies he followed all the years of his married life. As soon as he arose in the morning and had performed his morning ablutions, he began to recite speeches or to repeat poetry aloud. He walked the floor of his room as he repeated song after song, stopping now and then to fire some quizzing question, or some startling remark, for the entertainment of his wife, whom he equally delighted to puzzle and cheer. "Lalla Rookh," "Tam o' Shanter's Mare," "The Lady of the Lake," "The Cotter's Saturday Night," "The Relief of Lucknow," and a dozen more of what he deemed the masterpieces of poetry kept constant company with him in his bed-chamber. His beloved wife has said that she hardly recalls a morning of their home life when he did not greet the coming day with some verses or standard speeches. Generally he timed his dressing with the length of the recitation he happened to have in hand. Many a time his "guid wife," as he called her, would have to warn him that *his cakes* were growing cold while he was in the middle of his favorite recitation of Burns's "Land o' Cakes" or of the "Auld Meal Mill."

Mr. Dickson's temptation to the perpetration of practical jokes or to tease his best friends had many illustrations. They were never done in ill-nature, nor were any persons ever chosen his subjects for fun that did not possess his confidence and affection. Two weeks before his death he gave assurance to the writer of this memorial, in accounting for the many practical jokes in which he had victimized the friend he called his pastor, that these were only the foolish expressions and assurances of his love; FOR HE NEVER JOKED WITH THOSE THAT HE DID NOT PROFOUNDLY RESPECT.

We will record one illustration of this disposition to enjoy the discomfiture of his friends at the expense of his fun, and it will be one in the literary line.

Soon after Mr. Dickson became known as a public talker and a lover of books, he was invited to follow with a patriotic address a particular friend in a Fourth of July celebration in the town of Montrose, Pa.

His friend, afterward General Mylert, had then quite a reputation as a speaker, and was expected to deliver the principal oration. He had prepared himself accordingly, and had the full manuscript of his speech in his pocket. The two friends traveled up the mountain together on the day appointed. On the way Dickson noticed the roll of paper protruding from his friend's pocket, and, suspecting what it might be, he quietly transferred it to his own. While they rested at the hotel and waited for lunch, he hastily looked over the speech and said he liked it. When the public exercises began, he sat solemnly by the

side of his friend on the platform, who had no suspicion but that his manuscript was where he could
lay his hand upon it as soon as he should need it.
In due time he arose and began his oration. After
a few sentences spoken, he began to feel for his
paper, and found it was not in any of his pockets.
Supposing that either he had forgotten it at home,
or else that it had fallen out by the way, he boldly
struck out independently, and brought out all his
latent resources, with blunder and extemporary fervor. The embryo soldier and worthy patriot soon
found himself independent of all manuscript, and
carried the crowd with him, and so triumphed by his
very misfortune. After he was through, Dickson
was introduced to give the afterpiece in the patriotic
celebration. He arose, and with all the solemnity
of his father-in-law, Deacon Marvine, and after the
general style of that worthy, he drew the manuscript
from his pocket and read with great unction and
solemn earnestness the speech of his friend. His
style was so natural, and became so thoroughly
Dickson as he proceeded, without any reference to
the author, that he had given a considerable portion
of the speech before his friend detected his own
thought in the composition. It was so boldly and
cleverly done that his friend joined in the hearty
cheers with which the oration was greeted, and they
returned home together, splitting their sides with
laughter.

THE NEW YORK LIBRARY

...X AND
...NDATIONS.

Throughout life Mr. Dickson was a student of men and of principles, rather than of books. He treated those with whom he was connected in business or in social life as equals and associates, and he soon learned each one's personal peculiarities. His perceptions were quick and clear, and his judgments apparently without prejudice. The ability to weigh evidence and to balance probabilities on different sides of a business proposition, was unconsciously lost sight of by those who were his associates ; and perhaps was lost sight of by himself, in the readiness with which he reached his conclusions, in the clearness with which he announced them, or in the pleasant pertinacity with which he stuck to them after their announcement.

In the matter of writing papers he mastered the art of dictation. He used an amanuensis, and manifested a great ability to express all that he desired to express without the use of pen or pencil. His power of concentration in composition was remarkable. He could dictate letters and legal papers, apparently without previous arrangement or consideration, and sometimes carried on half a dozen subjects at the same time without breaking the continuity of thought. He was never known to make any study of the law. Perhaps he never read " Blackstone " in his life. But he possessed a legal ability, which he cultivated in his work, that was recognized by his associates as truly remarkable in his handling the immense business interests committed to him. He drew the most complex legal papers in which were involved the interests both of the " Dickson Manufacturing " and the " Delaware and Hudson " companies; including deeds for very large amounts of real estate, and contracts embracing millions of dollars. He was accustomed to dictate these papers with a comprehensive grasp and accuracy, and with a technical legal expression, which the best lawyers seldom attempted to modify. It was perhaps this ability to draw legal papers without the use of books, or the aid of learned counsel, which made the deepest impression of his great powers upon his associates in business. There were constant speculations among the higher circles of professional men touching this peculiar ability; as to whether it were a natural gift or a result of cultivation. His native honesty and his high sense of justice, between man and man, no doubt gave him clearness of perception in this direction. It was very seldom indeed that his embodiment of a business transaction did not entirely satisfy the parties involved, as well as stand the test of legal investigation. One of the best lawyers at the bar of Lackawanna County was accustomed to say that Dickson's legal papers were as good as he himself could draw.

Mr. Dickson's life was too busy to permit him to give his attention to that which he thought was the one bent of his mind, which was original investiga-

tion and literary composition. He said to the writer
of this, in the later days of his career, that he had
wasted his life, wishing and intending to write something that would live; but he never found the time
to begin. While making a tour of the world he
wrote a series of letters, which covered the impressions and observations of his wanderings; but these
letters were all directed to members of the family,
and were evidently not intended for publication.
After his return home he prepared a few lectures on
the different countries through which he had traveled, and upon invitation he delivered them publicly
in a number of places. But these were always given
on behalf of some benevolent cause, and generally
on behalf of the Young Men's Christian Association
in which he was constantly interested, and to which
he was a most generous contributor. He never
failed to gather a full house, or to entertain his audience; but it was generally thought that the attrac-
tion was the man rather than his lectures. He
himself found that in order to instruct and entertain
a promiscuous public, a study and practice were
required which he could not undertake, and that
possibly it required a talent which he did not possess. He was always most at home in the social
circle of literary friends, and in this he was the
most entertaining and instructive.

This much I have recorded of the book education
and the literary taste of this worthy man of remark-

able powers, as well as of conspicuous success. Thomas Dickson was never as strong or electric in his literary composition as he was in his extempore conversation. It was when his mind came in contact or in collision with other great minds that he sparkled and showed his really fascinating powers.

III.

HIS ORGANIZING POWER — BUSINESS ENTERPRISE — HONORABLE SUCCESS.

FROM the day that the boy Thomas mounted that unruly mule, whose mastery he had to make two attempts to establish before he succeeded in bringing him to his work at the mine-sweep, he entered upon his business career. He was small for his age; but his sprightliness, his neatness of habit, and his general good behavior had made him a general favorite in the village. As soon as it became known that he had left school and was looking for work, the best people of his acquaintance in the community became interested in his behalf. His first application was to the mine superintendent, very naturally, and he was successful in obtaining the only situation that could be given him at the time. He was, however, allowed to fill it for only about a week or ten days. Business men thought it a shame, or rather a waste of human resources, to keep such a boy guiding a beast, to draw coal by the bucketful from the mines. It was the performance of this work for a week, or ten days, which followed him all his life in the statement, never denied, that "he began his business career as a mule-driver at the mines." In a very short time, at least, Mr. Charles T. Pierson, a merchant of the town, offered him a place in his store, as a clerk and boy of all work. With this offer he went to his employer, and resigned his position at the sweep. The superintendent kindly dismissed him, and sent him to the paymaster for his wages. This paymaster happened to be Deacon Marvine, and the father of the little miss who in due time became Mrs. Thomas Dickson, and so shared all the trials and successes of life with him. The deacon congratulated his little friend on his finding employment worthy of his ambition and standing, and paid him an extra dollar for the excellent care he had taken of the animal committed to his charge.

This little incident brings to light a characteristic of the boy that followed him through life. This was his neatness of habit and purity of life. He would not drive even a dirty mule, if he had power to make him neat and tidy. He was a poor boy, indeed, but he was never ashamed to wear the coarse clothes which his mother prepared for him, and he kept them in such trim that no one thought of their coarseness. By his cheerful face and his natural manliness he commended himself to, and was readily received in, all the best society the village afforded. This habit of neatness followed him through life. While there was nothing of the dandy apparent in his youth, when he became a leader in the young society, nor anything of the fop suggested in his dress or taste when he sat at the head of the board, in New-York, guiding the immense business of a great corporation, his befitting dress and his neatness of habit always impressed all who came in contact with him.

It was not long after he entered Mr. Pierson's store before he found himself in the way of promotion. As soon as he made up his mind to become a merchant, he applied himself to the learning of the whole business. It does not now appear just how long he was with Pierson. The probability is that Mr. Pierson's business did not long require such an assistant as young Dickson proved himself to be. It is evident, however, that they parted with mutual satisfaction, for they were afterward associated in Dickson's great business enterprises, and were warm personal friends as long as Mr. Pierson lived; and Mr. Dickson was chosen the guardian of his estate and family after his death.

Mr. Joseph Benjamin about that time was one of
the largest merchants in the village; and Thomas
entered his employment and very soon became his
most trusted clerk.   He identified himself with all
his employer's interests, and by his popular ways,
both in and out of the store, became a most efficient
helper in the business.   His rapid and steady progress in reaching the position of a popular business
young man was generally recognized, and his worth
was very early felt in the community.   This was
evinced by the fact that when, after a couple of
years, Mr. Frederick P. Grow bought Mr. Benjamin's store, he made it one of the conditions of the
purchase that Thomas Dickson should go with it
and enter his employment.   While Dickson could
not exactly consent to be sold with the goods, his
attachment to the store led him to go with it.   For
two years he became a member of Mr. Grow's family, and stood with him at the head of the business.

Mr. Grow was a man of high honor and excellent
business integrity, who needed just such an assistant.   He was also a Christian gentleman of most
genial spirit, and a very faithful friend.   The friendship formed between these two young men became
one of the conspicuous and beautiful features in the
life of each.   Dickson's attachment for Grow never
weakened or faltered.   If we may judge by the test
that Dickson intended to give when he said he never
teased anybody whom he did not love, or if the

amount of his teasing was in any proportion to the
measure of his true affection, it is perfectly evident
that Frederick P. Grow and his excellent wife were
special objects of his confidence and love through all
the years of his life. Mrs. Grow seems, from the beginning, to have adopted the head clerk of her husband's
store as the child of her heart, and always appeared
to be most happy when taking a motherly care of
him. Even down to the day of his death her interest
in him continued, and Mr. Dickson's funeral presented
no more touching scene than that of this woman, in
her widowhood, weeping over his fallen tabernacle.

Thomas Dickson was born with a facility for making friends, and equally for holding them, when he
had once attached them to himself. His friends, in
all his business life, were found among all classes
and conditions of men. The intelligent and the
humble, the day-laborer and the associate in his
office, and the representatives of rival industries, all
seemed to be personally attached to him, and took
every proper opportunity to show him their confidence and love.

About two years after Mr. Benjamin had sold out
his store to Mr. Grow, he again entered the field
with a much larger and more general stock of merchandise. He purchased the foundry, which had
been set in operation a few years before, and included a drug department in his promiscuous store ;
and so prepared himself to meet the general wants

of the community. Mr. Dickson had taken good
care of his salary, feeling that he owed it to his self-
respect, as well as to his family, to confine his
expenditures within his income, and, as far as possible, thus be ready to contribute his portion toward
the help of his parents in any family burdens or
exigencies which might come upon them. By an
economy which never suggested stinginess, he had
been able to save something for capital; and he now
especially wished to try his hand in business for
himself. About this time his grandfather, whose
name he bore, sent him an earnest invitation to visit
him in Scotland, and accompanied the invitation
with the money necessary to meet his expenses on
such a visit. Thomas placed this money in bank,
and after careful consideration determined to deny
himself the visit, until he could get more fully upon
his feet. Finding that Mr. Benjamin wanted his
services in his new store and general enterprise, he
proposed to go in with his old friend as a junior
partner. This proposition was readily accepted, and
Dickson entered the firm by placing his grandfather's gift, with all the ready money he could raise,
in the business. This proposal thus accepted, he
at once took special charge of the drug department; but very soon became head manager in the
store, giving as much time as he could to the details of the foundry. The business was quite successful, especially in the direction of the foundry;

and gradually both partners turned their attention to the development of this department of their business, leaving the store more generally to the management of reliable clerks, among whom were his brothers John A. and George L., who in a few years became partners in the concern; and both entered upon a most successful business career for themselves. Mr. Dickson continued in this business with Benjamin up to the spring of 1856, some ten years after his marriage, prospering in it throughout most of that time.

By this time the industries of the coal-field had reached a second stage in the measure of their development, and gave dim prophecies of their future greatness. The Lackawanna valley was still a wilderness, with its dense forests of pine and hemlock. Its pure streams were filled with trout, while deer from the mountains were to be seen now and then on the outskirts of the small settlements. The iron-works established by "The Scrantons and Platt" in the Slocum hollow had struggled through many disappointments and hard times, and especially through the failure of their expectation in the effort to develop what they then supposed to be the real wealth of the valley. They had placed their iron-works alongside of the outcrop of anthracite coal, within plain sight of the immense mineral wealth which invited their enterprise; but it was with the persuasion that the bog-iron ore found here

and there in small quantities, and the abundant tim-
ber at hand for feeding a charcoal furnace, and for
the supply of a good lumber-mill, had opened for
them a highway to wealth.

The Delaware and Hudson Canal Co., organized
many years earlier, with its management in New-
York and its field-center at Honesdale, in its attempts to operate in the valley of the Lackawanna,
had found immense difficulty, with limited success,
in its management.   The early operators in anthracite coal all had to learn wisdom by the hard way of
experience, as had the pioneers in all other enterprises in the country.   The amazing devotion of
American genius to the mechanic arts, which, in a
single generation, has produced its fruitage in the
immense progress of invention, which has revolu-
tionized the world, and the ages, had at that time
hardly begun.   The master mechanic of this greatest
coal company of that day was a worthy millwright,
puzzling himself alternately in a wilderness of imperfect or untried machinery and of unknown wants and
indefinite necessities.   The chief leverage for lifting
the treasures buried hundreds of feet under-ground
had been the pulley and sweep operated along slopes
with a motive power of mules and horses.   Only such
coal veins as were above water-level could be worked,
as no adequate machinery had come into the field for
the clearing of the mines of water.   The exhaustless
power for pumping out and working these mines

was yet to be found in the streams which came sing-
ing down the mountain-sides, or lay like ribbons of
silver in all the valleys. These mountain streams,
with their banners of vapor in the frosty air, were
ever suggestive of the unmeasured service ready to
be bestowed on him who should discover and harness the latent forces, which thus far had been wasted
all over the world on overshot and turbine wheels.

The power of steam had indeed been discovered,
and venturesome men had invented imperfect machinery for its direction and use; but the difficulties and
drawbacks were immense, and the capital both scarce
and very timid.

It was in the midst of these difficulties, and right
along the line of this highway of slow development
and of immense outlay of capital, of patience, and of
industry, that the path of young Dickson lay, as he
brought his brains and honest purpose into the field
of enterprise and labor. As soon as he had become identified with Benjamin in the foundry at Carbondale, the enterprise of making tinctures and
molding pills, whose virtues he tested on green
clerks and inquiring rustics, for the amusement of
young men, became entirely too small for his
thoughts and plans of life. His thoughts began to
turn toward the necessities and uses of machinery
for the development of the coal enterprise, which his
foresight told him must be immense, in the near
future. The success, in a limited way, of the Benja-

min foundry suggested to him a larger enterprise in
this direction, and he longed for the possession of
such a field of work, in which he could himself be the
leader; one which might in time provide the machinery already needed, and which he foresaw must be
needed in increasing quantities throughout the valley. It required at that time a whole week to travel
from the coal-fields to New-York, or Philadelphia.
The transportation of supplies, or of machinery, was
exceedingly slow, laborious, and costly. Through
much of the way this transportation had to be by
wagons, with mule teams, on roads, too, almost
impassable. Added to this was the difficulty of con-
structing or improving machinery suitable for the
necessities of the work, so far away from the field of
operation. All these facts weighed upon the active
mind of young Dickson, until at length he determined to attempt the organization of a manufacturing company under his own control. He at once
brought to this purpose his peculiar talent for
utilizing the human forces within his reach. He
enlisted his father and his brothers, and then his
partner and some of his associates in the village,
and put his whole force into the organization of this
scheme. After he had settled upon his plan for the
organization of a partnership company, and had
induced his father, James Dickson, and his two
brothers, John A. and George L., who had become
interested with him in the store, to unite with him as

far as they were able in the venture, he then interested the two brothers, Charles P. and Morris Wurts,
and with them Messrs. Joseph Benjamin, Peter J.
Du Bois, Charles T. Pierson, and John Dorrance. All
of these men had been more or less intimate or
associated with him in the struggles of their earlier
life and business. These all joined in the enterprise
as silent partners, and placed their money, to a limited amount, in the firm which was established under
the title of " Dickson & Company."

Thus a great and permanent industry was started
in the valley by the foresight and energy of this
young man while the dew of youth was yet upon
him ; and with its growth and efficiency he has ever
been identified. In the early spring of 1856 this
enterprise took practical shape. In April of that
year the organization of this company was definitely
effected as the recognized business of " Dickson &
Co."; and Thomas Dickson was chosen its active
manager. After a careful study of different locali-
ties, touching their advantages for such a plan as
was proposed, and considering their promises of
future success to the industry which he had determined to inaugurate, the young manager, then
thirty-two years of age, concluded to establish
his plant at Scranton, which had already begun
decidedly to grow, under the wise management of
the Lackawanna Iron and Coal Company. He was
doubtless influenced to this decision, in some meas-

4

ure, by the prospect of railway connections, which promised better at that time for this point than for any other in the valley. He acted promptly as soon as his mind was made up, as was his habit. He purchased for his site a number of acres on what was then known as Pine Brook, at the point where it emptied into the Lackawanna, and close by the village graveyard. Thus early he began the work of interesting the members of the Lackawanna Iron and Coal Company in his scheme. As soon as this purchase was completed from that company, he sent down from Carbondale a sturdy, hard-working Scot who called himself Sandy Turnbull, who had applied to Mr. Dickson for work of any sort. As soon as the frost permitted he, in the spring of 1856, began to dig for the foundations of the new shop, whose future success was destined to carry the Dickson name over most of the continents. This same Sandy Turnbull spent his life running the main engine of the shop, with whose noise and song he forever mingled his praises of Thomas Dickson, his employer. He seemed to think he was still working for "Tomus," as he called him, years after Mr. Dickson had finished his work and gone to his rest. To this faithful Scot it will be glory enough for this world if he should learn that his name had occurred in a memorial of Thomas Dickson.

This venture of the Dickson Company proved generally successful, and throughout its history it

SCRANTON FOUNDRY AND MACHINE WORKS.

DICKSON & CO.

THE NEW YORK
PUBLIC LIBRARY

ASTOR, LENOX AND
TILDEN FOUNDATIONS.

has been one of the potent forces for the development of the Lackawanna Coal enterprise, as well
as in securing the growth and blessing of the city
of Scranton. On the 1st of May, 1862, the company was reorganized, enlarged, and chartered as
a stock company under the law of Pennsylvania,
under the name, style, and title of "The Dickson Manufacturing Company." This company was
named for Thomas Dickson, its founder, and he was
chosen its president and sole acting manager. With
energetic fervor and careful industry Mr. Dickson
pushed this enterprise and met with rapid success.
His two brothers, John A. and George L., and his
sister's husband, John R. Fordham, quite early became identified with him in the works, and two of
them continued with the shop long after he had left
its presidency. His friend, Charles T. Pierson, after
the stock company was established, came to Scranton
to represent the Carbondale stockholders in the practical conduct of the business. But for years the
controlling stock was in the Dickson family, and the
president never lost any of the confidence which
these worthy business men reposed in him. "The
Dickson Manufacturing Company" built locomotives
for the railways and engines for the mills and mines.
They constructed all kinds of machinery for the manufacturing industries of the rapidly forming companies and developing business enterprises all over
the country, east and west. They constantly en-

larged their shops and facilities until, in the locomo-
tive department alone, they were capable of completing two locomotives every week, and their
stationary engines and machinery found ultimately
a world-wide market.

In the presidency of this successful enterprise
Thomas Dickson was succeeded, as time passed,
first, by his brother, George L. Dickson, then by his
daughter's husband, Colonel Henry M. Boies, and
then by his eldest son, James P. Dickson ; each of
whom enlarged the capacity and efficiency of the
works. The company still continues to operate under
the management of James P. Dickson, and bids fair
to carry the name with honor through the business
schemes of coming generations.

The Delaware and Hudson Canal Company became one of the chief supporters of the Dickson Manufacturing Company very early in its career, by the
purchase of its products. Indeed, its general transportation superintendent, Charles P. Wurts, and a
number of its employees were stockholders in it.
But the directors of that corporation became friendly
to its enterprise, first, through the excellency of the
work it turned out of the shop; and then by the
business honesty manifested by the young president
and manager. This historic canal and coal corporation had found immense difficulty in developing their
coal enterprise, which was perhaps increased by the
distance of the headquarters of the organization from

its field of operations, as well as from the hindrances
of imperfect transportation.   The general panic and
business disturbance of 1857 brought to this company, as it did to all great corporations, immense
perplexity and trouble.   From the entanglement and
depression of business, in which the disturbance of
the country was almost universal, the Delaware and
Hudson corporation recovered but slowly.   The
"Manufacturing Company" under Mr. Dickson's
management came to their help as far as it was possible.   He aided the company in various ways, both
for the sake of his own enterprise and theirs, and so
attracted responsible men toward himself and his
manufacturing interest.

At length, in the summer of 1859, Mr. George T.
Olyphant, then President of the Delaware and Hudson Company, came to the valley for the purpose of
putting the field management into a more efficient
condition.   James Archbald had resigned his position as coal superintendent a few years before, to be
succeeded by John and James Hosie, in their order,
each of whom, after a short service, had left the field
to undertake other important enterprises.   During
the interval, and up to this time, Charles P. Wurts,
Superintendent of Transportation, had had general
charge.   He was a most efficient officer, who had
completed the Gravity Road, built to connect the
company's canal at Honesdale with the field of operation in Carbondale, and was now preparing to leave

the country for a sojourn of some years in Europe
in the enjoyment of his private fortune.　While here
Mr. Olyphant met Thomas Dickson at the time he
was perplexed with this condition of things, in which
he felt a personal responsibility, and was impressed
with the conviction that it would be the best thing
for their enterprise to get him interested in the
canal company.　After consideration he offered to
him first the place of coal superintendent, and then,
as soon as Mr. Wurts should have withdrawn, that
of general superintendent or field manager for the
Delaware and Hudson Company.

This was a decided advance upon any position
Mr. Dickson had yet occupied, and involved a large
addition both of work and responsibility; but he
believed himself by his knowledge and energy capable of fulfilling its duties.　After a careful consideration, with his characteristic and transparent honesty,
Mr. Dickson agreed to enter the service of the
company, with the proviso that he should be permitted to retain his position at the head of "The
Dickson Manufacturing Company," and at the same
time hold the Delaware and Hudson Company, as
formerly, a regular purchaser of the products of their
shop.　This, of course, was a condition which could
be permitted only upon a conviction of the highest
integrity in the manager.　It must give power to
the salaried officer of the coal corporation, in some
measure, to use his position for the enlargement and

prosperity of another corporation, in which both his money and his reputation were involved. But the Delaware and Hudson Company seems not to have hesitated to accept these terms. They made the appointment. This was the highest compliment they could have paid to the integrity and manliness of Thomas Dickson. Nor did they ever have reason to regret the trust they reposed in him. They placed him in this position of general manager in the summer of 1859, and allowed him to supply the field necessities of the corporation from the machine-shop which he had established and had fully in hand. Thus Thomas Dickson became identified with this great coal and transportation company, with whose subsequent growth and history he was to become so conspicuously identified.

For ten years Mr. Dickson held this double position, becoming constantly more burdened with its work and responsibility. The enlarged schemes of both companies called for the highest and most conservative financiering ability. The outbreak of the civil war had proven an unexpected stimulant to all business enterprise. In nothing was it more powerful than in the iron and coal departments in which Mr. Dickson was interested. The demand for the anthracite coal, and for machinery of all sorts, constantly enlarged throughout the four years of the war. Both the coal-mining of the valley and the work of the machine-shops were doubled in a very short time, and this gave Mr. Dickson immense increase of work and responsibility. There was not only the work of the day to be done, but foundations wisely to be laid for future enterprise. There were coal-lands to be discovered, the various strata developed and tested, and leased or purchased. There were breakers to be located and built, and these to be furnished with the best machinery. There were immense transactions in real estate, in which titles were to be traced through tortuous lines of early history and made secure. There were homes to provide for under-officials and laborers. There was live stock, in the way of hundreds of horses and mules, with all the supplies and equipments necessary to their efficient use; and with these the immense care included in the active superintendence and control of miners, and other employees of all sorts. Then along with this multiplied trust was the operation and care of fifteen miles of gravity railway, with its lifting-engines, and the supply and protection of the company's canal from Honesdale to tide-water. The care and management of all this work Mr. Dickson undertook, and was successful in it, while he still held his responsible relation as President of the Dickson Manufacturing Company, which he had already led to what he felt to be an assured success.

Of course it was impossible for any man directly to manage all this multiplied work; but Mr. Dickson developed and manifested a power and genius in his

management that few men ever reach. In these two
positions he applied and demonstrated his native
endowments, and especially his ability to select, to
harmonize and use any number of subordinates with
the smallest amount of friction, and so as to secure
the best general results. His judgment was so clear,
and his conclusions so fortified and distinctly announced, both to his associates, subordinates, and
employers, that they seldom needed revision. He
was said to be a stubborn man, and probably he was.
But he always gained his points with the best of
good nature, and his triumphs left those who were
discomfited by him without lacerated feelings. Indeed, generally men became his better friends after
their differences with him. He once said to me that
he attributed the best success of his life to his ability
to control men without requiring them to feel it. His
efficiency in managing the great trusts he had held
he traced to the facts that he always treated his
subordinates as his friends; always personally received them as his equals, just as far as they would
allow him to do so; and that he tried his best to
deal justly with men, in every condition of life.

Mr. Dickson continued to hold his double trust in
the complex position as president of the manufacturing company and coal superintendent of the Delaware and Hudson Company up to the first of May,
1867, when the business of both companies had so
enlarged that the burden of responsibility became

too great, he was persuaded, for a single administration. He had associated with him those who
had become fully prepared to take up his work
for the manufacturing company; and therefore he
resigned his office as president of that company in
favor of his brother, George L. Dickson, who had
proved himself entirely worthy of the trust. He
continued in the Board of Directors, and kept his
stock and interest with the company as long as he
lived. He now became fairly enlisted and fully identified with the Delaware and Hudson Company. He
established the offices of the company in Scranton, in due time, on the adjoining square to that
occupied by the manufacturing company's shops.
The railway was built from Carbondale to Scranton,
with branch roads and tracks to all the breakers of
the company, as soon as these were completed. A
new road was also constructed, as a branch from
Green Ridge, to connect with the Lehigh and Sus-
quehanna, and the Jersey Central, at Wilkes-Barre.
To serve the best interests of this great corporation
now became the prime object of Mr. Dickson's life.

As soon as he concluded to make Scranton his
home, he began to identify himself also with the
interests of the young city, both in a social and business way. He united with the most energetic business men, and the best citizens, in the effort to
provide the city with all necessary public institutions, Christian and moral, as well as with such as

might concentrate capital and facilitate business. On the 20th of September, 1863, in company with half a dozen other leading citizens, he united in organizing the "First National Bank of Scranton," which has proved, throughout a period of more than twenty-five years, one of the most successful institutions of its kind in the country. Mr. Dickson continued in its board of directors as long as he lived. By his conservative force, and justice in dealing, he endeared himself to all his associates in this enterprise, and did much toward determining its business character.

On the 22d of April, 1865, he also associated himself with a number of gentlemen of the city in organizing another industry in the valley, which was destined to become one of the institutions of the country. This was the "Moosic Powder Company," the special reason for the organization of which was, no doubt, found in the enormous amount of blasting-powder necessary to be used for mining purposes in the valley. As one of the founders of this enterprise, Mr. Dickson continued in its board of directors throughout his life. This industry has prospered for many years, and continues to increase its product and enlarge its market. The clearness of Mr. Dickson's foresight and his sterling business ability might be reasonably inferred from the more than ordinary success of the business organizations in which he was an actor or leader, and from the abundant and lasting fruits of their enterprise. There were many of these with whose initiation he was identified, which were more or less successful. Indeed, as a general thing, those of them which were farthest removed from his influence proved the most hazardous and the least successful. As he rose in his business position, and his characteristics became more widely known, he was chosen to one directorship after another in the great organizations for business in New-York and Scranton. Some he accepted and some declined; but the great service of his life was given to the Delaware and Hudson Canal Company until he became almost its embodiment as well as representative in the public mind.

After seven years' service as general superintendent of this corporation he was elected its vice-president in 1867. Two years later, in the summer of 1869, he was chosen its president. In this office he continued through more than fifteen years, and only vacated it at the summons of the Angel of Death.

Thus for almost twenty-five years of full and active service in the three highest places of trust in the Delaware and Hudson Canal Company, this boy of the mine-sweep with its unruly mule, gave to the great corporation his energy, his genius, and ability, and he died beloved by all who worked with him or under his direction. The estimate of his associates in the directorship, and of the stock-holders, of his character, both as a counselor and a man, will be perpetuated to his family in the papers placed upon the records of the company, some of which will be incorporated in this memorial.

IV.

HIS HOME AND HUMOR — HUSBAND, FATHER,
FRIEND — SOCIAL LIFE.

IT will be borne in mind that it is not proposed
to write any adequate record of the acts and
business schemes of this successful father and friend.
It is not intended, in any proper sense, to present or
preserve a view of the material harvests of his sow-
ing. We are not able to trace the manifold results
of the forces which he set in operation in his more
than ordinary business career. It is the man and
brother, with his clear head and true heart, which
we are seeking to embalm in his household and
among the circle of his friends and associates. His
business career and his great enterprises are supposed to be useful in this direction only in so far

as they reveal his genius, for clear apprehension, and his manly rectitude of character; only in so far as they intelligently illustrate his success and his life of honest justice, or reveal his great heart of generous benevolence toward men of all conditions. What he did for himself, for his family, for his associates, and for the world at large, shows him to have been worthy of the greatest honors and the tenderest remembrance his posterity can ever give him.

But it is in the home, the social and religious life of the man, that we discover the most precious characteristics, which ought to perpetuate the memory of this home-made and loving character. About the time when young Thomas Dickson came out a full-fledged clerk in the Carbondale store, and began to try his talents in debating clubs and literary societies, he started to win his position in the social life of the young people. The winter singing-schools offered just the field for his enterprise, for there was real music in his soul, although a music which could hardly be set to the peculiar square notes of the music-books then in use. During the recesses and breathing-spells of this semi-social and semi-musical soirée young Dickson was accustomed to bring out his best parts in social episodes to the music, for the refreshment of the girls. Just for the fun, he exercised himself in the effort to carry off the most sprightly lass who happened to have company whom he judged not exactly to her liking. It gave quite a zest to the life of the settlement to witness these contests of gallantry between the young men. The community thought it no harm to laugh over the discomforts of the spruce young man who had settled himself under a profound conviction that a certain young lady only waited the crook of his elbow to allow him to exhibit his proficiency in gallantry, when he found, after he begun to crook that elbow, the smiling miss was decidedly leaning toward the rollicking clerk of the village drug-store. To "cut out" somebody, as it was called, was better to Thomas than the rhythm of song, and to take home some "other fellow's girl" afforded the appropriate music for his step.

It was in the midst of this kind of harmless mischief that Thomas found his destiny at last. In one of these scouting adventures he snatched from the approach of a young man, who had been foolish enough to make public his intentions, the sprightly young daughter of Deacon Marvine. The name of this young lady was Mary Augusta, the eldest daughter of Roswell E. Marvine and Sophia Raymond. Mr. and Mrs. Marvine were known as two of the most devoted and consistent Christians in all the valley. They were natives of the State of New-York, and had moved into the valley about the time the work of coal-mining began. Mr. Marvine soon became one of the trusted agents of the Delaware and Hudson Company. He was chosen a ruling elder in the

Presbyterian Church, and his excellent wife became
the leader in the Christian society of the community.
They were blessed with five children, all of whom
afterward reached stations of influence and Christian
efficiency. The eldest girl of this excellent household,
which was known for fifty years as a leading family
in the valley, was this Mary Augusta, whom Thomas
Dickson approached at the breaking-up of the sing-
ing-class and offered himself as a substitute of some
worthy young man whom he thought not quite good
enough for her. She accepted his gallantry for reasons best known to herself, and on the walk homeward the congeniality of spirit seemed so complete,
and the fitness of things so surprisingly natural, that
Dickson ever afterward maintained that it was during this same walk that he determined to win the
girl's heart and marry her sometime if he could. It
seems, too, that Miss Mary could think of no vital
objection to this scheme of the young man if he
should conclude to undertake it.

Mary Marvine was a very sprightly, amiable girl,
endowed with as many Christian virtues and maid-
enly excellencies as could be desired. Domestic in
her tastes, and uniformly amiable in temper, she was
thought in the village society to be possessed of
all the virtues of that womanhood which promises
to make a man's home blessed. Her whole future
proved that these prophecies were certainly true.
At the age of fourteen years she united with the

Presbyterian Church by profession of faith, and
through all the years of her consistent after-life she
has proved the sincerity of her profession.   It was a
striking incident that Thomas Dickson and his sisters united with the same church on the same day
with Mary Augusta Marvine.   Before these two had
any thoughts of uniting their hearts and destinies
for the pilgrimage of life, they had begun their
Christian walk together.   Miss Marvine was between
sixteen and seventeen years of age when young
Dickson began his attacks upon the citadel of her
heart.   The result was a foregone conclusion among
their friends from the beginning, and the suitable-
ness of the match was generally acknowledged, and
nobody knew how to prevent it if it had been other-
wise.   On the 31st day of August, 1846, when she
was barely twenty-one, and he not yet twenty-three,
Thomas Dickson and Mary Marvine were united in
marriage, bearing with them into the new life the
best wishes of a host of friends and the respect of a
whole community.   They immediately set up their
housekeeping in a humble way in a rented house
in Carbondale.   From the beginning Mr. Dickson
manifested his domestic tastes as well as his ability
to make his home cheerful and happy.   The little
house became a rendezvous of the best young society,
and Dickson's cheerful ways and fun-loving disposition was allowed its full play, sometimes to the
amusement of his nearest neighbors.   Even the few

moments of the noon hour, which the young husband
snatched from his work, were filled with shouts of
laughter in the home where the young wife found
her special enjoyment in those arts and cares that
make a home delightful. Their life was so full of love
and interest to themselves and to their associates
that those who met Dickson in his home scarcely
ever thought of him as a man burdened with great
schemes or responsibilities.

He never carried into his home any of his business
cares. This rule he followed throughout his busy life.
His wife even yet says that she can recall but a single
instance when the immense burden of his business
was not left entirely at the office;—but one instance
when he was actually kept by the cares of that business from his usual peaceful sleep. That was the time
when his associates in business seemed to have lost
both their faith and courage. He felt that he stood
alone with the night of disaster closed about him.
He had pledged his entire fortune in the faith that
the company, for whose character he stood, would
be able to weather the storm of the financial disaster which was working ruin of business trusts everywhere. When he closed his office and turned his steps
homeward, as long as he had good health, he seemed to
gather mental elasticity and vivacity as he approached
his family. By the time he had reached his door
he was all ready to quiz his wife, or astonish his children with his preposterous pleasantries, which opened

their young eyes with wonder — pleasantries he had
invented with the aid of his fruitful imagination.

Genuine Christian hospitality became the expression of his home, whether it was the little cottage
kept with careful economy, or the great house in
which luxury glorified the success of honest business,
in all the loving life of this husband and wife together.   They seemed most happy when they were
sharing the good cheer of their home with their
friends of all conditions of life.   They spent a respectable fortune in the expenses of their free hospitality, and in it all there was never a suspicion of
vanity.   Success in life awoke no spirit of vanity, in
either husband or wife, who had so cheerfully walked
the paths of poverty and rigid economy together.
Experience, in which the enjoyment of prosperous
life and the ability to gratify their own tastes by the
increase of income, had indeed taught them the real
value of money ; but it brought them no temptation
to start upon that way of economy whose goal is
narrow meanness, which is called " the charity which
begins at home." The husband and wife were always
one in the conduct and enjoyments of their home-
life and its hospitality.   Rich and poor, the refined
and the uncultivated, when they crossed the threshold of Thomas Dickson's dwelling found neither the
spirit nor the conventional forms which might suggest to honest souls the possibility of intrusion.   His
wife used to tell, as an offset to some of his innumer-

able drives, when he attempted to tease her about
her personal tastes toward certain people, a story
which illustrates his native sympathy with humanity
and his real democracy in spite of himself. He was
affected with the almost universal social prejudice of
Americans against the colored race. Now and then
he essayed earnest argument with his wife on that
subject. His wife had inherited from her father that
broad humanity which finds no ground for disrespect
in the mere color of the African's skin. Now and
then she would threaten to invite a colored man or
woman from their neighborhood to dine with the
family. He used to answer, "Well, ' guid wife,' you
may invite them, and eat with them, if you feel called
to do so. You may give them the best you have,
and I shall be happy; but I will wait patiently until
they are all through. Or, if it will be more convenient, I will eat in the kitchen, and they shall have
the best of the house; BUT EAT WITH A NEGRO I
NEVER CAN,—at least, not until he grows white and
loses his odor." At length, one day Mrs. Dickson
was more than surprised to see her husband bring
home with him, upon an invitation to dinner, one of
the darkest of the race, in his working-clothes. She
remonstrated, of course, with great earnestness, with
the fun dancing about her eyes; but he protested
"this was no ordinary negro. He was one of the
most honest, real white men he had met with in
years"; and he insisted that he should be placed

next to his host, and make the children wait if they did not like it. She mentioned the possible odor which she feared might interfere with the comfort of his dinner. But he insisted that so godly and honest a man as this could have no odor about him that a true Christian should object to. In fact, he thought him simply a colored Scotchman. The family, of course, complied with his wishes with a suppressed pleasure which was highly spiced to them by the anticipated privilege of the advantage he had afforded, and which they should not be slow to use in their spars and drives with him in their future discussions of this colored question. But henceforth he never alluded to the subject voluntarily except to frankly acknowledge, when reminded of his weakness in company, that once in his married life his wife had got the better of him; and he said he could see no reason why she should not, when she had been so unfair as to train all her children to help her. His ability to free himself from difficulties and uncomfortable positions, whether in social or business life, was as striking as the sharpness and wisdom of his care to avoid them. He was seldom nonplused by an opponent, and if he were, he did not forget it, but good-naturedly "bided his time" until the opportunity of balancing accounts came to him.

As soon as it was determined to establish the Dickson Manufacturing Company at Scranton, Mr. Dickson decided to move to that place and identify

THE NEW YORK
PUBLIC LIBRARY

ASTOR, LENOX AND
TILDEN FOUNDATIONS.

THE HOMESTEAD, SCRANTON, PA.

himself with the growing interests of that young
city. Here, in the autumn of 1857, he purchased a
house, which was then new, but which since has
been greatly enlarged and improved, and which still
stands at the corner of Washington avenue and Vine
street. This house for more than twenty years has
been known as the Albright residence, the house
in which Joseph J. Albright, Mr. Dickson's choice
friend, lived and died. Into this house Mr. Dickson
moved as soon as he had established the machine-
shop, a little more than a square away from it. In
this house some of his children were born, and the
family became attached to it by many happy associations; but it was too small for Mr. Dickson's
enlarging hospitality and increased responsibilities;
and especially too limited to meet the necessities of
his growing family. He lived here for five years,
during which time he built his large and luxurious
residence on the adjoining grounds. This house,
which he built on Washington avenue, has stood for
years as one of the beautiful homes of the city.
One of Mr. Dickson's chief reasons for building was
the want of room for improvements of his family
home which time might demand, and especially want
of grounds for the exercise of his taste in landscape
gardening, which in the later years of his life became a solace and a luxury in which he delighted.
On the Christmas day of 1862, when the country
was in its great struggle to subdue the slaveholders'

rebellion and save the Union, the family moved into
this, the only house which he ever built for himself.
From time to time he enlarged and improved it, and
now and then lived in other places, but it was always
considered the family home.   Here Thomas Dickson
set up his Penates and sanctified his home life with
his family altar.   This was the home which he filled
with the choice treasures of his taste, and crystallized
them all with his peaceful family history.   From this
family altar, fortified by a Christian mother's care,
his children went and came, threading the ways of
their liberal education.   Its shadows were made
sacred by the members of the family circle who
grew weary and left it for "the rest that remain-
eth."   From its threshold went forth the grown-up
children, with their father's benediction; held in
the bonds of that new life which breaks and forever
enlarges the family circle.   Innumerable remembrances of the happy household are treasured within
these walls, within its halls and airy chambers.   But
among all its precious treasures there remains the
one figure—the husband, the father, and friend, forever the most precious and sacred to those who
remain on earth.

The later years of his life, after his children were
married or had scattered, the pressure of business
compelled Mr. Dickson to reside for part of the year
near to the headquarters of the company, in New-
York.   Some winters he consequently spent in hotel

life, always occupying the same rooms at the Gilsey Hotel, where he was inseparable from his wife. While here he exercised his hospitality as best he could; but growing weary of this kind of life, he followed his home tastes, and purchased a beautiful residence at Morristown, N. J., with its adjoining grounds of fifty acres, more or less. This he called his Jersey farm, and in nothing did he ever find a way so fully to gratify his taste, or to enjoy the peace and comfort of his home-life, as when he walked or rested among its flowers and magnificent trees. He never seemed more happy than when pointing out the pictures of peaceful beauty to the multitude of his appreciative friends who perpetually gathered about him. His friends and associates all reached the one conclusion, that whatever might be Thomas Dickson's grasp of mind, or his power to mold men and control business, his special endowment was his ability to create and beautify a Christian home upon earth. Along with this was the power to tie humanity to himself and his household with the bands of intelligent, generous affection and lasting friendship. With the warm heart and straightforwardness of the child he blended the truthfulness of the just man in all his home life as well as in his business. Hence it is that most of his friends remember him not specially as a great and successful man of business, who by the versatility of his genius and patience of his industry arose from

the narrow life of poverty and uneducated youth to
win a magnificent fortune single-handed, and make
a place for himself among gentlemen and scholars of
the best station on earth; but rather as the husband,
the father, the citizen, and friend, walking among
the flowers which he planted as if he had been born
there. He never seemed so great and good as when
giving his time to eliciting and enjoying the wonder
of his grandchildren who clung to him. The real
manhood of the successful president was most conspicuous as he sat under his own vine and fig-tree
to entertain and enjoy the converse of the number-
less friends who had learned the way to his heart
through the loving hospitality of his beautiful home.
It was Dickson the Man, the Brother, rather than
Dickson the President and broad-gauged man of
business, that had made for himself a place in the
hearts of the men of his generation. Yet there
were few men of his generation who ever carried
heavier business schemes to such certain and permanent success. It was his chief excellence that he
never permitted his business to swallow up or sully
his beautiful manhood.

V.

RELIGIOUS FAITH AND ITS EXPRESSION.

OF the religious character and life of Thomas Dickson it remains to make some worthy record. This portion of his memorial I approach with some hesitancy and diffidence, which arise, not from the specific case, but from the general subject. There can be no desire to place upon this family tablet any of that pious literature of the cemetery which certainly is apt rather to preserve pictures of the living than excellences of the dead. It is a difficult thing to record justly and truthfully the Christian character of a brother who has gone to his account. We cannot speak of that character as we could if he were present to modify or protest. But if any man is able to make a fair record of the Christian faith or of the religious life and character of this man, it would seem that the writer of this memorial ought to be able to do so. During the last sixteen years of his life, in his private intercourse, he was accustomed to recognize him as his pastor as well as friend.

Yet there is so much in the intercourse of a Presbyterian Christian and his pastor which contains in it heart-history, ever to be held sacred, that no account could be honest or full which records religious life or convictions as fully known between them. There is a vast deal of personal experience which can never be brought to the light of the world. Then, too, there is so much in the burdens and trials of a busy public life to interfere with that which Christians are wont to conceive as the only consistent exhibition of what they call religion, that it is difficult for a conscientious pastor to give even his own clear judgment of the spiritual life or Christian excellence of his friend. The world and Christians have such different standards of judgment, and the best men have so dim a perception of the true excellences of Christian character and the worthy proportions of Christian zeal, that it becomes perplexing even to attempt to draw a positive picture of one which may satisfy the outside world and do strict justice to the subject.

But this we can say, and be sure that the Christian world who knew him will both understand and fully appreciate it: THOMAS DICKSON'S RELIGION WAS

A LIFE which was founded and built upon what is understood as the evangelical orthodox foundation. It was a grand principle running through his modes of thought, his pious meditations, and his business activity alike. He was neither in his business nor his religious life subject to moods of either ecstatic feeling, or spasmodic activity. His Christian life and virtues blended so naturally with his daily dealings with men, that he seemed never to step into a new atmosphere, or change his step, for the performance of religious duties. He was subject to no periods of doubt and dullness of spiritual apprehension, nor to spasmodic acts of piety in order to heal soul-bruises arising from an irreligious worldly conformity.

At the age of sixteen years he gave his heart to his Saviour, just as his parents had taught him he should, and in a time of special religious interest in the community on the subject of religion, he took his place, with many of his young companions, in the Carbondale Presbyterian Church, upon the profession of his faith. From that day, we will be safe in the conclusion that he never once thought of taking back, or modifying, or of denying his confession of Christ. It was a hearty and true confession. He never became what we would call an aggressive Christian; perhaps with his special endowments and life associates he could not have been; but his clear conception of the method of grace, and his final settlement of the great questions of the soul's salvation,

left him with few anxieties in regard to his relation
to God with which his life might be clouded. For a
time he once became entangled with the discipline
of his church upon the vexing and never-settled
question of youthful and social amusements. On
this subject he and the Carbondale Session could
never agree; but with a manly, Christian spirit he
maintained his position, which his best friends believed to be right; and he patiently waited until the
views of the Church itself brought him out fairly into
the light. He was a supporter of the Church in
every possible way, and brought up his family to
venerate all its institutions as well as to bear its
burdens with a manly honesty, which he never could
call generosity or benevolence, but simply Christian
duty. The proper expenses of the Church to his
mind never came under the head of benevolence;
and if he ever failed in his patience toward his
fellow-Christians at all, it was toward those who
delayed or neglected to do their duty in the bearing
of church burdens.

Through his whole life Mr. Dickson was connected
by membership with only three churches. The Carbondale Presbyterian Church, of which both his
father and his father-in-law were ruling elders, was
the one where he confessed his Lord. After years
of connection with it, he transferred his membership
to the First Presbyterian Church of Scranton, after
he moved to that city. In this church he early be-

came a leader, and remained in its communion until it was found wise to send out a colony for the founding of a new organization in the growing city. He was appealed to to become the leader of this colony. In this movement he hesitated, believing it to be premature. But after receiving the assurance from his pastor and friend of his judgment that he ought to lead the enterprise, and after extracting from this pastor the promise that the bonds of friendship and of pastoral association should never be weakened or broken by his new church life, he consented to go with the colony to form the Second Presbyterian Church of Scranton. In this organization he remained a leader and the largest contributor until he entered the Church of the first-born, whose names are written in Heaven. In this church he proposed to give one-tenth of all that was necessary to be raised for the church building or for benevolent purposes. The organ in this church, presented by his widow, bears his name upon its front, and stands before the church his perpetual memorial.

His association with the brethren in all his church life was happy, being always without the suspicion of arrogance, or any demand of recognition, because of either his wealth or his business position. He was but a member in the church in all his association with God's people, and asked for no higher place.

Wherever Mr. Dickson remained for a time, either

in his summer vacations or winter work, he identified himself with some congregation of evangelical Christians, and became more or less intimate with the pastors; and many a country church and pastor felt the benevolent power of his sojourn. When in the city of New York he always held a seat in one or more churches, and became intimate with their pastors. During two or three years he held a pew in the Reformed Church. His friend Dr. Ormiston, a brother Scotchman, was the pastor. With this pastor he heartily associated through all the later years of his life, and he had no dearer friend or warmer admirer. When he took possession of his home at Morristown he identified himself with the church of which Dr. Erdman was the pastor, and while still retaining his membership in the Second Church of Scranton, he was ever recognized in Morristown actively interested in their church work. Dr. Wm. C. Cattell, for years the President of Lafayette College, was for years recognized as one of Mr. Dickson's most intimate friends. He and Dr. Erdman, together with Dr. Ormiston and his old friend and pastor in Scranton, found the Dickson residence the home of a parishioner. At his death these four ministers of Christ mourned for him as for a brother.

He seemed really to have had few if any temptations to exercise himself with questions of a speculative faith; nor did he have very profound convictions of the importance of any logical system of theology. His piety was never expressed in theological terms, nor was it manifestly molded into a dependence upon forms of worship. In a word, his religion was to be found in his life—adorned by his exercise of the Christian virtues of justice and generosity to all. It was expressed by his brotherly kindness and charity, in his contact with the world under all circumstances. His piety was recognized in the manifest sincerity of his reverence for everything sacred, and in his spirit of humility in all his dealings with God and with God's people. His family altar, his Sabbath observance and public worship were but the unostentatious and regular fulfillment of Christian duty, as he understood them, and apparently as much so as the payment of a debt or the meeting of a business appointment. His support of the church and his contributions to church work were constant and generous; and he usually aimed to use his contributions so as to make them a power to increase the benevolence of others. While a great deal of his benevolence was spontaneous, he generally gave away his money upon Christian principle, and very seldom from impulse. He was an enlightened friend of colleges and institutions of learning; but he never had the time to abide long enough in a college atmosphere to become actively identified with this grand power of Christian civilization. He always seems to have been interested in

6

the work of Christian churches in the community
where he happened to live, and in the endowment
of Christian institutions wherever he was brought
into contact with their work and saw their need;
while he never became greatly interested in the
great work of missions among the heathen. His
life was too largely concentrated, and too thoroughly
identified with the opening business of the great
country in which he lived for him to enter fully into
the spirit of missions to the race, as conducted by
the great Church he loved.

While Mr. Dickson was never aggressive as a
Christian in the sense of commending the gospel in
words, or religious appeals, he was never indifferent
to the salvation of men's souls; nor did he ever hesi-
tate to express his religious convictions on all suitable
occasions. He had a very dear and life-long friend,
whose bent of mind, and habits of thought and investigation, led him into the fields of religious doubt
and speculation, respecting the Church and the tenets
of the Christian faith. Dickson's association with this
friend was, through many years, the most intimate and
brotherly. To all his friend's speculations he used to
answer, with the same clear and positive conclusion
which characterized him in business propositions,
somewhat after this style: "My friend, we know very
little of the things that are beyond the limits of our
senses; and I am entirely confident that after we have

learned all we can, and speculated as far as we please, we shall have to come back honestly to the exercise of the same faith in the Redeemer of mankind which our fathers had, and simply trust in Him for our salvation, unto all eternity."

His attendance on public worship was precisely of the same regular character as his appearance in his place of business. No amount of burden or care, no whims of taste or weakness of the preaching, were ever allowed to prevent his appearance in God's house among the worshipers.

The illustrations of the decided practical character of his every-day religion are abundantly scattered all along the path of his Christian life. I will record a single one which certainly deserves to be perpetuated.

On the 16th of November, 1873, the congregation of the First Presbyterian Church in Scranton celebrated its twenty-fifth anniversary. The exercises of the morning were under the direction of the pastor, who devoted the hour to a historical discourse, which included in it the early history of the city as well as of the church, and which proved refreshing to all the old citizens. In the evening the congregation took the matter into their own hands. Papers and speeches containing reminiscences and historic gems were presented by the laymen, both old and young. In the afternoon, between the morning and evening services, the pastor received the following note, which explains itself, and which we think belongs properly to this memorial. It was as follows:

SCRANTON, Nov. 16, 1873.

MY DEAR DOCTOR: During your very interesting review of the history of the church, this morning, the thought occurred to me that something might be done to give prominence and abiding interest to the occasion.

I suggest, therefore, that an endowment fund of $10,000 be raised, which shall be permanently invested by the Session of the church,— which can be securely done at, say, 7 per cent.,— and that the income arising therefrom be held and used by the Session for the relief of the poor of the church, and for no other purpose. The annual income would be $700, and in a community like ours might be productive of much good. While we are having a love-feast and general shaking of hands, let us do something that will be approved by those who are to follow us, and which the Master we profess to serve enjoins— "*take care of the poor.*" If this suggestion meets your approval let the movement be initiated, and, if possible, be completed to-night.

I am aware that, in the present conditions of the financial and industrial interests of the country, all feel poor, and that the present may be considered an in-opportune time ; but the money will not be needed at once.   Let the subscriptions be made bearing inter-est at 7 per cent., so that there may be immediate income, and payments of principal be made hereafter, when money is more plentiful.   We ought to be will-ing to incur debt in such a cause.

If the project meets approval, I will subscribe $1000 provided the full sum of $10,000 is raised.   If you think well of it, I will see you during the afternoon.

Very sincerely yours,

REV. S. C. LOGAN, D. D.   THOMAS DICKSON.

The pastor read this letter to the evening congre-gation, and followed it with an address, in which he heartily indorsed the proposition it contained as both appropriate and opportune.   He proposed that this memorial of God's grace, recorded in the history of the church, be raised at once, to mark this historic point in the life of this remarkable organization. This proposition was at once accepted by the people, and in a very few minutes more than $7000 of the $10,000 proposed was subscribed.   Mr. Dickson then arose and proposed to increase his own sub-scription to $1250 if the amount first proposed could be fully raised that night.   The congregation took him at his word with a glad enthusiasm, and in just

12 minutes from the time the subscriptions began, as indicated by the pastor's watch,— which he held in his hand,— that subscription was completed, and a fund to provide for the poor of the church was established amounting to $10,830.

The pastor then announced to Mr. Dickson that the terms of his proposal had been met. He thanked him for this suggestion and his generosity to the poor, and called upon him to know if anything remained to meet the conditions of his own subscription. Mr. Dickson in an appropriate acknowledgment stated his reasons for making his subscription conditional, through the hopes of completing the work at once and having a monument erected in the history of the church. He hoped the subscription would be left open, that none of the members might be deprived of the blessing of taking a part in this good work, if they should choose to do so. He closed his remarks with his subscription of $1250. This fund for the poor was Dickson's pious thought; and it was just like him. His piety led him in all his career to be mindful of the poor. With the poor his early life was associated, and as, step by step, he rose, he carried the poor with him. Through all time this monument of Christian love will stand, with its beautiful proportions, a way-mark in the work and history of this remarkable church of Presbyterian people. And the most conspicuous names on it, associated with those of the noblest men and women recorded in the

history of the city, to be read by the Lord's afflicted
disciples, are those of Thomas Dickson, and of his
wife Mary.

Mr. Dickson's benevolence was generous and without ostentation. He was never heard to claim any
sort of credit for what he gave, nor to ask for any
special consideration in any of the churches where he
identified himself with God's people because of what
he was able to do for his Lord and Master. Thus
we ever conceive of Thomas Dickson's religion — as
practical, without the suggestion of ostentation. Its
life-principle was to be found in all his walks and pur-
suits, so constant and noiseless as to be thought simply a part of his life's business. His utter incapacity
for cant, or pious expression, taken with his fun-loving
spirit and his identification or association with men of
all sorts, possibly sometimes placed him, in the minds
of earnest Christians, as one possessed of no great
depth of religious feelings ; but his pastor and friend
ever found, in the depths of his honest life-experience,
the pure gold of a loving Christian heart. The testimony of his associates and co-workers was given with
singular unanimity to this fact, when they recorded
their estimate of him after he was gone.

We can speculate upon what might have been his
power, and his wider influence as a Christian or a
religious man, if his environment had been different ;
or if he had consented to the desire of the church,
more than once expressed to him, to accept the

office so long held by his venerable father. What he might have been in the courts and great schemes of the church, had he become a ruling elder, we who knew him might reasonably conjecture. We may imagine that for many of the duties and responsibilities of this office he was both richly endowed and well adapted; but, doubtless knowing himself better than his friends could know him, he decided wisely in declining all positions in the church save those of a sincere and faithful membership. His association with ministers was never with them as a class, while he listened with pious regard to all of them, and with a catholic spirit. But many of his choice personal friends and associates were ministers of high standing, for whom he cherished the affection of a friend rather than the interest of a parishioner. These servants of God he has bound to himself and his family by cords of love and precious remembrance of kindness which his death has only made more permanent in their hearts. Such of these ministers as are alive to-day count it one of their choice blessings in life that God gave them an intimate association with Thomas Dickson and his Christian wife.

Thus I have tried to give a true and general estimate of the life and character of a man whose memory must ever be precious to those who knew him, specially so to those who were bound to him by the ties of kindred or blood. On every branch of the sub-

ject that has been considered, whole volumes might
have been written. I have simply attempted to give
glimpses, or passing shadows, of the successful business man who was, and must remain, in the memory
of his associates a noble father, husband, and friend.
There is presented here only outlines and incom-
plete figures which his children may perfect, in order
to secure the remembrance of the full-rounded man,
with his full-rounded life, who now rests from his
labors; while his life-blood and the fruits of his
industry work on to bring blessing to their lives
through the ages. On each of these specifications,
facts and incidents are abundant that would certainly
be of interest, and might be indefinitely multiplied
by his friends. But it must be remembered that this
tablet is only intended to be suggestive to that circle
whose life has been identified with his. It will have
met its end if it shall prove helpful in recalling and
perpetuating the remembrance of the many-sided
and graceful endowments that, as a Christian man,
he unconsciously exhibited to the circle of which he
was the life.

Thomas Dickson never worked for posthumous
fame, nor thought to live up to a possible obituary
which his friends might give him. Weaknesses
he had, but why should we remember them in
our estimate of his well-poised character and successful life. These weaknesses only endeared him
to sensible men, because they were glorified and

transmuted by the excellencies that all knew to be precious. He was religiously a straightforward, believing sinner, who assented cordially to whatever he recognized as God's appointment; and with his last breath he expressed his creed in the sentence, " It is all right." It now remains for me briefly to record his declining life, and the Christian dignity with which he went to his rest. This, with some of the testimonials and estimates of character that were the chaplets of affection with which his business asso-ciates adorned his tomb, will complete his memorial.

VI.

DECLINING HEALTH—TRAVELS ABROAD—FADES AWAY
—PASSES THROUGH THE TWILIGHT TO
THE MORNING.

MR. DICKSON was never what would be called a robust man. Physically, he developed very slowly through his boyhood and youth. Light and wiry in his boyhood, he began life for himself at so early an age that he seems to have been imbedded in the memory of his early friends as "Little Tom Dickson." This impression appears to have been carried forward with his after-development, and he became stereotyped in the minds of men generally, perhaps, as below the standard of the physical manhood of the stalwart generation to which he belonged. This, however, was a mistake. When he reached his manhood he stood about five feet ten and three-quarter inches in height, and was remarkably straight and well-proportioned, as well as elastic in his carriage.   Through the first half of his life he was blessed with almost uniform good health, and certainly had great powers of endurance.   A staid and indefatigable worker, his life-long habit of spicing his labors with the luxury of his fun seems to have rendered his business life uniformly pleasant and healthful.   He was able to pass from outdoor activity to office confinement with the smallest appearance of friction, and he never seemed to carry about him any nervous anxiety or bustle of business. His powers of endurance and general good health seem to have educated him to the neglect of any special care of himself in this matter.   The multiplicity of his business, the hardness of the work, and the dangers of exposure seem to have been seldom thought of by himself as elements to be considered in his decisions concerning the demands of duty. The buoyancy of his nature and adaptability of his physical manhood, which we might call his nervous force, continued, with few interruptions, down to the beginning of the year 1863, when approaching his fortieth year.

In the early part of January of that year, he was driven and weighted with more than his ordinary business.   In addition to the care of the rapidly increasing responsibilities of the great company, of which he was the chief factor, he was called upon by

public officials, and by citizens generally, to aid in the
perplexities of public affairs which were incident to
that period of the war. During the whole four years
of struggle and sorrow in the country he never declined any service which the exigencies seemed to
require of him, whether of council or sacrifice. At a
time when he was in a condition of physical exhaustion and mental weariness, he was suddenly called
from his home to a council of patriots in New-
York. Taking the Delaware, Lackawanna and Western Railroad to Great Bend, he entered a train on
the Erie road late at night, and, without observing
his surroundings, he sat himself down among a
crowd of Confederate prisoners that had been cap-
tured in Virginia. This was just after the great bat-
tle of Fredericksburg. Here in his weariness he fell
asleep, without thought or care of his fellow-passen-
gers. As soon as he was discovered by the con-
ductor of the train he was hurried into another car;
but it was too late to escape the consequences of his
exposure. He pushed his business through in New-
York, and returned home with all speed and without
rest, but he came from his second night's travel with
a fever which in a few days developed a genuine
case of small-pox, which converted his beautiful
home, for a time, into a pest-house, in which his wife
was established in all the offices of nurse, steward,
and cook. After the regular process of the disease
he came forth with few external signs of the plague,

but with a grasp of disease about the valves of his
heart, from which he was never afterward entirely
free.   He was soon found in the full harness of enterprise and business at his office, but his vigor and
power of endurance seem to have been visibly weakened.   He suffered from painful and strange attacks
of exhaustion, shortness of breath, and sensations of
brain confusion, which to his wife and family became
alarming.   These attacks were not particularly vio-
lent, and they were at long intervals, which perhaps
became the more wearing on his general health and
spirits from the mystery of their cause.   This cause
was only fully and clearly revealed after his death,
twenty-one years after the first appearance of the
symptoms.   It was the slow and very gradual ossification of some of the valves of the heart.   It was so
gradual, that for at least ten of the twenty years he
lived after this siege with the small-pox, he did not
think of himself as really out of health.   But his
great labors gradually told upon his strength and
elasticity, as became apparent to his best friends.
He was observed to use his carriage more frequently, and when he walked he manifested a delib-
eration and dignity of carriage which could hardly
be supposed to be the signs of approaching old age.
Yet these things gave no suggestion of real disease.
His responsibilities, with the confinement incident to
his business, after a few years began visibly to wear
upon his health.   After his election to the presidency

of the Delaware and Hudson Company his best friends began to discern the signs of approaching prostration, and they begged him to desist and take a rest in life's labors; to cut himself loose from the harness in which he had pulled from his childhood, and try the effect of general travel.

Both his reading and his interest in the world's condition made these suggestions pleasant to him, as he considered them. He turned his thoughts to the outer world, with which he had been in more or less direct contact through his business, and expressed a growing desire to see how other people lived, at home.

The Company at length took the matter seriously in hand. They gave him a year's leave of absence for travel and recuperation, with the expression, on the part of the directors, of their best wishes for his restoration to health. So he determined upon a tour with his "guid wife" entirely around the world. His eldest son, James P. Dickson, had been for two years residing at Hong-Kong, China, and perhaps this fact, in good measure, determined the direction of his route and the length of his journey. As his health had become somewhat precarious, his beloved wife became the more constant companion of all his travels. Indeed, he became inseparable from her after his children had begun to walk alone through the world. While he perhaps never acknowledged to himself that his mysterious disease had anything

to do with keeping her with him, it nevertheless became very apparent that he wished to be near her,
whether at home or abroad.   In the midsummer of
1871 he reached his conclusion to make the long
journey—taking his "guid wife" to see her boy, as
he said, on the under-side of the footstool.

About the first of September, 1871, Mr. Dickson
left his home in Scranton thus accompanied by his
wife, going westward to make this tour of the world.
On the 24th of that month they arrived at San Fran-
cisco, and sailed from that port in the steamship
"Republic," on the 28th, for the port of Japan, and
from thence to Hong-Kong.   In China Mr. and Mrs.
Dickson were joined by their son, who journeyed
with them and returned home with them to remain.
They passed through the chief countries of Asia.
They traveled through Syria and Palestine on horse-
back.   They climbed the Pyramids of Egpyt, and sailed
up and down the Nile together.   They threaded the
narrow channels of the historic islands of the Mediter-
ranean, sailed along the borders of Asia Minor, and
thence back through the islands of Greece into Italy.
Here they met friends from home, and with them
made the tour of Europe, using every sort of con-
veyance.   They passed through Italy and climbed
the mountain passes of Switzerland.   They drove
through Germany, stopping to drink life-waters from
the medicinal fountains.   They looked into the gay
life of Paris and the more substantial one of Lon-

THOS. DICKSON.

1883.

.. NEW YORK
UELIC LIBRARY

A OR, LENOX AND
T..D..N FOUNDATIONS.

THE NEW YORK
PUBLIC LIBRARY

ASTOR, LENOX AND
TILDEN FOUNDATIONS.

don, and then passed northerly through England, and reveled among the historic hills and valleys of Scotland, in midsummer. They visited all the points which had been deemed sacred around the fireside of the emigrants in the far-off new country, and traced the foot-prints of their fathers through Scotland and northern England; thence they passed into Ireland to visit what Mr. Dickson calls "the land where my masters come from,"—referring to the great number of Irish laborers it had been his life-work to employ and to serve. The tour of Scotland, Ireland, and England was completed toward the end of August, when they sailed from Liverpool on the homeward voyage. They arrived safely at home on the 27th day of August; thus having encircled the earth in just about the space of one year.

During this whole year of travel Mr. Dickson's health seems to have improved, and his enjoyment to have increased with his progress. From the start, he adopted the plan of letter-writing to his family and relatives at home, giving thereby an accurate account of his travels and impressions. These letters were forwarded with business regularity, containing accurate pictures of the lands he visited ; but among them, ever visible, was the unconsciously-drawn picture of the traveler himself. They were written in all manner of straits and with every conceivable inconvenience, but they were masterpieces of personal

7

correspondence. These letters were preserved, and afterward collected and bound in a book constituting 276 pages, foolscap size. They were never intended for publication, but they remain a family souvenir, containing a great amount of knowledge, and many marks of literary ability, as well as of an accurate observation. They are filled with the sparkle of their author; and those who knew him, as they read these pages, can see the twinkle of his eyes and hear the droll announcement of his observations, whether among the Chinese, the Arabs, the Turks, the Italians, or Caledonians, as distinctly as if they were with him.

This year of relaxation proved a great benefit to Mr. Dickson in various ways. It enlarged the man; gave him better views of life and of humanity, and increased his business capability. But his most intimate friends were still oppressed with convictions that his physical manhood had received a shock somehow, and that he would probably never enjoy the buoyancy of health which had marked his early career. By the time he had crossed the continent in his departure, the return of his physical vigor and his mental vivacity gave to his friends the confident prophecy that restoration and prolonged life lay in the line of the travel he had chosen; and there can be no doubt but that his life was prolonged a number of years by this timely rest from work.

September, 1872, found Mr. Dickson again in the harness, ready for the greater burdens which in his absence had been taken by the Company. The long line of railway connecting the Company's coal-fields with the Dominion of Canada had been undertaken and pushed well on toward completion, and this added greatly to his cares and responsibilities; but he took up the additional work without hesitation, and completed this international enterprise. This, because of the condition of the business of the country, led him and the Company into a labyrinth of difficulties through which he struggled for the next few years in a way that illustrated his highest business qualities, and out of which he came with an illustrious reputation.

The rapid developments of the country had, through a series of years, tended to the extensive enlarging of all schemes of business. Corporations which had started from small beginnings had become greatly enlarged in their operations, and seemed constantly, and in some cases unreasonably, to be reaching forth toward all schemes of business enterprise. The necessary consequence of their success was that they began to overlap and entangle each other. Complications of business and the clashing of enterprises became frequent, and general. The whole field of associated capital became the more hazardous and perplexed; possibly by reason of the steady increase of the financial depression which affected the whole country throughout the period from 1872 to 1878. Over-production seemed to have accumulated supply far beyond the proportions of demand, in the market. Uneasiness and depression, in time, smote all business circles, and with greater or less power disturbed the peace by destroying that confidence among men without which successful business is impossible. There has been in the history of the industries connected with the anthracite coal-fields no period more trying, nor one in which higher mental and moral qualities were demanded, in order to save the great corporations from wreck, and successfully carry forward their enterprises. This was the period in which Mr. Dickson demonstrated his highest powers, by his adaptability of wisdom and honesty to the necessities of the times.

He had but fairly entered upon his charge, on his return from abroad, when this period of long and perplexing trial came upon the Company of which he was the president. Here was the exigency under which his greatest qualities of mind and heart were most distinctly demonstrated; where both his genius, his wisdom and his poise, founded upon his unshaken faith, proved of inestimable value.

It is not the intention of this memorial to write a history of these years of the great clash of industries, whose causes it would be difficult if not impossible exhaustively to trace. Of these I have treated, at some length, in the work styled "A City's Danger and Defense." Here it is enough to say that these financial complications culminated in the unparalleled strike of 1877, and the temporary confusion of business throughout the whole nation. For a time the business of fifty millions of people was dependent upon the whim of an organized multitude of railway and manufacturing laborers, who, in defiance of law, attempted to control the great industries by a concerted strike. We will not even attempt to chronicle the exigencies of the Company with which Mr. Dickson was identified, nor the trials through which it passed as a consequence of this strange complication and depression of values. It is enough to say that this old and responsible corporation, for a time, was watched by anxious friends much as a ship that is discovered among breakers in the fury of the storm, with sails torn and ropes broken; as a ship when the crew and subordinates are seen to give more attention to the life-boat than to the ship, whose doom seems almost certain. But through all the rage of the waters this calm, cheerful captain is visible, standing unmoved and collected, as the prophecy and assurance that the ship shall yet weather the tempest and ride clear of the breakers. President Dickson pledged all he had in the world to save the Company, with whose life the fate of so many widows and children was involved; and then brought to its service all the latent powers of his honest nature and versatile genius. His wisdom and integrity; his sense of justice and his faith in God; his sympathy with his fellow-men of all ranks, and his persevering hopefulness, shone out through all these years; and they leave for us to contemplate the very embodiment and expression of a true Christian manliness. His plans and his influence swept out silently and persistently until their power was felt in the whole field of the coal and railway industries. "Patience" had "her perfect work," and when the high seas subsided after the storm, and wrecks were strewn everywhere, this master anchored his charge in the haven of success without even the suggestion to the outside world that any extraordinary skill or courage had been required. He was never known to urge any claim for personal recognition because of these services.

But these were years when there was great waste of vital energies and expenditure of physical force. Mr. Dickson kept up his vivacity and his cheerfulness. The world in which he moved saw little change in him, save that which was conceived as simply natural decay of human life. Some even charged him with heartless indifference, because he walked so calmly and cheerfully through the ordeal. But his loving wife crept nearer to his side under the increased burden of care and apprehension. Somber shadows fell on the inner circles of his friends, who thought they discerned him in the grip of some mysterious disease. Through all these years his power of will, and his high purpose, kept him in regular step with the march of his duties; but when the day was over he sought more earnestly for quiet, and showed his need of rest not to be mistaken. It always seemed so easy and so natural for him to make everybody happy and cheerful about him; and it seemed so unnatural for him ever to complain, that it was not until his end was almost at hand that his associates could think him seriously disabled. He kept his great work fully in hand up to within a few weeks of the close of his life. Yet it was discovered, after his death, and announced by his physicians, *that " his life for the last ten, or fifteen, years had been hanging upon a thread."* His activity under such a pressure of disease was more than a marvel. The ossification of the valves of his heart had gone on steadily through the course of years, limiting the flow of blood in his system, until, when death came, an orifice through which a cambric needle could hardly be passed was the last channel left for the vital flow.

In the spring of 1883, under the urgency of his family, he left his office. For three months he rested, and traveled with his wife and some of the younger members of his family. With a few friends he sailed for Europe in the early part of May. He spent the summer chiefly in travel, by private carriage, through England, Scotland, and in different countries upon the Continent. This relaxation he greatly enjoyed, though constantly burdened with physical weakness and suffering. His observation seemed to be quickened, and his love for his old friends seemed to grow stronger as the shadows gathered about his life. With his son for his amanuensis, he rested himself from the weariness of his travels in writing letters to his old friends at home, in which his life-long wit and wisdom flashed out with their wonted vigor.

He returned in the autumn to his post, but took hold of his work with a weary and relaxing grasp. Through the long winter following he toiled without complaint, while his family and friends schemed together to relieve him of his heavier burdens, and absorb him in the enjoyment of social life, with the hope that he might yet find rest, and recuperate. But he calmly and hopefully faced the reality of life's issues, and silently determined to fall at last in the harness of business, which had never galled nor fretted him. His intellectual force and mental energy never seemed to flag, nor to weaken. His wit and his love of fun kept full step with his patience and dignity, and so continued as long as he lived. When in the spring and early summer his physical weakness shut him up in his summer home at Morristown, or confined him to the walks over his beautiful grounds, he amused himself and his friends by making his little granddaughter his special nurse and equal companion. Little Ethel Boies became his matron and teacher. She told him when to get up and when to retire. Showed him how to put on his clothes in the

THE NEW YORK
PUBLIC LIBRARY

ASTOR, LENOX AND
TILDEN FOUNDATIONS.

RESIDENCE, MORRISTOWN, N. J.

morning, when he always seemed to have forgotten which side of the garment went before, and which behind. With loving patience the little one changed for him his shoes, that always seemed to be seeking for the wrong feet. She showed him how to shave and comb his hair when he seemed always, in a puzzled way, to take the hair-brush for his razor and always hopelessly mixed the soap, towels and water. He was never too weary to puzzle the child and watch her motherly care develop. She became his companion, and among the full crop of June roses of the Dickson home there was nothing more beautiful or enchanting than this mingling of the graces of sunset and sunrising. Never was decaying manhood, after a full life of vigor and success, made more beautiful and precious than when thus glorified by its mingling with this lovely childhood — a childhood which followed it with the patience of love and a constantly increasing puzzle of wonder.

Mr. Dickson still superintended his work in his feebleness, and fulfilled the duties of his office with the aid of his associates up to July. He continued to pass up and down the railway, in answer to the claims of duty, with his loving wife at his side, seeking always to gather and dispense cheerful comfort. He visited his children and relatives in Scranton and Carbondale in midsummer, and made his last public appearance at the marriage of his sister's daughter, Miss Mary Fordham, in Scranton. He still walked

erect and greeted his friends with his life-long hearti-
ness.   But he seemed ever conscious of the rapidly
approaching dissolution.   At his last appearance in
his Scranton office he made his old friend and pastor
sit down with him at his desk, and for an hour held
heart-communion with him on the solemn side of the
drama of life, with its mysterious close in death, and
its revealed eternity.   In it all he spoke with the
same calmness which characterized his business activity.   With simple trust in the Saviour of sinners,
he said he proposed to walk on until he should fall,
trusting that, when he did, the good and merciful
God would take him to the home of eternal rest and
full satisfaction.

He returned from his farewell visit to the scenes
of his youth, and of the responsibility of the riper
years, to his home at Morristown; and after remain-
ing a few days passed up the Hudson, still able to
do light duties, and hopeful of continued strength.
While on this visit at the Catskill House he was
taken suddenly worse, and his attack was aggravated
by the fact that he was out of reach of his physician.
With much difficulty he was taken back to his home at
Morristown.   Shrinking from the idea of helplessness,
he doubtless by his very physical exertions aggravated his attack, and hurried on the exhaustion which
was so rapidly pushing him out of the world.   Leaning on the arm of his old friend, Coe F. Young, he
even protested that he was giving assistance, rather

than receiving it ; and found breath in the very limits of his life to cheer this life-long friend and brother. Poor Young had to laugh through his tears, while Dickson persisted in twitting him with his clumsy helplessness and dependence upon the friend he had leaned on so long. His cheerfulness and his mental vivacity were the last signals he left flying in the view of his life-long friends who gathered about him. His Morristown pastor, Dr. Erdmon, sat down by his bedside and found the solid comfort of a soul implicitly resting in hope ; and discovered the real heart-strength of the Christian, which gave blessed token of a coming glory.

Without a complaint, or disturbed confidence for a moment, Thomas Dickson sunk away with the declining sun of the afternoon of the 31st of July, 1884, when, as the evening shadows began to lengthen, he passed through the twilight to the morning. Suddenly the "wheel was broken at the cistern," and this noble brother, husband, father, friend—this man of successful business, whose life was so precious to so many other lives—simply "fell on sleep" and "was not, for God took him." He had gathered his garments about him and lain down, with Christian dignity, to his rest.

VII.

VOICES OF THE NIGHT — SYMPATHIES OF HUMAN
BROTHERHOOD — FLOWERS WET WITH TEARS.

THE shock of President Dickson's departure was
felt, far and near. Through a thousand hearts
in the fields of life and activity the wounds from
broken heart-strings showed how he had gathered
humanity into loving association with himself. As
the sun set and night gathered upon the home
where the broken-hearted Mary Marvine, with her
great love, so long his companion, must henceforth
walk in her widowhood, the pulsations of grief were
found knocking at every door, laden with tokens of
sympathy. Families all over the communities where
they had lived had been watching at the bedside of
the dying man as, hour by hour, the telegraph and

telephone told the story, and the steps, of his decline. The voices of sorrow trembled and broke silently about the stricken household. Here are some of these expressions of sympathy and grief, which testify of the character of the dying Christian, as well as give glimpses into the hearts of those who were soon to follow after him. The selection of these expressions has been made by Mrs. Dickson herself, as mere specimens of the sympathy of human brotherhood which flowed in as living streams to mingle with the floods of household grief. They are but voices of the night sent to cheer and strengthen the weary souls that sit in its darkness. They are as follows:

SCRANTON, PA., July 30, 1884.

Mr. JAMES P. DICKSON, Morristown, N. J.

My Dear Friend: While I know that both you and your father's family are assured of my profound sympathy at all times of trouble, I feel to-day that I ought to send to you a simple reminder, if, possibly, it might make your burdened mother feel just a little stronger to bear her burdens to know that she does not suffer alone. There is but one sentiment in this community to-day, and especially among the people that you and I are acquainted with. It is one of the deepest sorrows of our life that a man of such excellence as your father must go away to return to us no more.

Words in such a case as this, and at such a time as this, lose all their force, and silence always seems to me more potent and becoming than speech. I can only say I loved your father with a feeling which began in admiration of his honest, manly spirit, and was strengthened by every contact with him through a long series of years, and which is made the more sacred by a deeper conviction of his real Christian character. It is a great thing for a Christian to live such a life as he has, in the midst of such temptations, and under the burdens of such a stewardship as he fulfilled. But it is a greater thing for a Christian to die than to live. " Precious in the sight of the Lord is the death of his saints." Of all the voices of Providence or of the Holy Spirit for which your father has listened in the perplexities of an honest, conscientious life, there is not one that contains in it so much of unspeakable comfort and joy as that which I presume he shall hear to-day, " Well done, good and faithful servant."

Please assure your mother, on any suitable occasion, that Mrs. Logan and myself weep with her, and cease not to pray for our dear Lord's presence with her in these waters of affliction, for whose depths we have no measure. The Lord only can comfort her; and He can do so.

If your father and my friend is conscious when

this comes to hand, please give him my undying love; and ask him now and then, in the joys of the Father's house, if he shall find room for it, to recall this poor sinner, who has been associated with him so long, and who hopes to meet him soon on the banks of the river of life that flows from beneath the throne of our Father.

If I can at any time be of use in this sorrow of your home and house, I will be happy to have you command me, with all freedom. Give yourself no trouble to acknowledge this note; it is only the outgoing of a lonely heart in the day of your trouble, and needs no recognition. God bless your mother and her children.

With sincerity and grief I am your and your father's friend,   S. C. Logan.

Whitby, Ontario, Canada, Aug. 1, 1884.

Dear Mrs. Dickson: The sad tidings of your bitter bereavement have overwhelmed us with sorrow. I only wish I could go and silently mingle my tears with those who mourn for him to-day, and personally assure you of our deep and tender sympathy with you in your grief. Your noble-minded, generous, warm-hearted husband was very dear to me. My heart went out irresistibly toward him. I loved him as a brother, and as such I mourn for him. I will cherish his memory while I live, and I pray God I may, through riches of divine grace, be permitted again to renew our intercourse in that home where death never enters.   I have been suffering much this week, and am better to-day, but my physician enjoins quiet.   Had I been able to undertake the journey I would have gone to Scranton on Monday, as my heart prompted.

May the richest consolations which the gospel of Christ presents be yours in this your time of need. As your day, may your strength be.   Mrs. O. joins me in loving sympathy to yourself and kindest regards to each of the several bereaved households. May the God of the Fatherless bless them all.

Yours very faithfully,

W. ORMISTON.

EDINBURGH, SCOTLAND, Aug. 16, 1884.

MY DEAR MRS. DICKSON: The letter from your son James which I received last Tuesday ought to have prepared me for the worst; but when I learned to-day from Mr. Wood, who has just joined us here, that my beloved friend is no more, the blow seemed as sudden as if it had come without any warning, and I am overwhelmed with sorrow.

I need not refer to the great loss which the public has sustained by the death of one so honored, trusted,

and useful in the many important enterprises with
which he was connected; nor to the loss of the
Church by the removal of one who in private life and
in his prominent public position so honored the doc-
trine he professed. Still less would I dwell upon
your own great sorrow. That is too sacred for any
words of mine. I can only, out of a full heart, commend you and your dear children to the consolations
and support of our Heavenly Father. But I may
speak to you of my own personal loss, which I feel
to be irreparable. I shall never find another such a
friend. At my time of life new friendships are seldom formed; and then, where could I hope again to
find a man like him? Mr. Dickson must have known
that I respected and loved him, but I can scarcely
think he knew the strength of my attachment. He
had many devoted friends, but among them all, I am
sure there was no one who more lovingly or more
continuously kept him in grateful remembrance than
I did. Since he bid me good-by on the deck of the
steamer last October there have been but few days
when some loving thought of him has not been in
my mind, and I cannot now repress my tears at the
thought that I shall not receive his greeting upon
my return home.

But may God give me grace so to live that I shall
yet receive from my beloved friend "welcome home"
when the voyage of life is ended; if through Christ's
love I may reach that blessed and peaceful shore,

8

where your precious boy has already welcomed his father, and where, in the joy of God's presence, they both wait for you.

Mrs. Cattell sends her love. She, too, feels the sense of a great personal loss in this bereavement. Again I pray that our dear Lord may comfort and sustain you, and that He may help us all to bow with reverent submission to His holy will.

Faithfully your friend,
W. C. CATTELL.

These are but a tithe of the great love-expressions that came to this stricken household as the night of bereavement fell upon it. Heart-expressions of grief and sympathy, mingled with honest, manly testimony to the great and good life just closed, were poured into this "house of mourning" by the hundred from all parts of the country. Weeping women wove crowns of glory with choicest flowers to place upon his narrow house, and wet them with their tears. Devout men in all walks and business of life turned aside from their accustomed paths, and gathered to bear away his body to its resting-place. Strong men, churches, benevolent societies, and great organizations, betook themselves to the weaving of chaplets of sincere and manly testimony to his excellence and his genius, with which his tomb should be crowned.

The press of two continents, as the telegraph announced the departure of his soul, sent forth the
record and estimate of this man of business whose
genius had been illustrated by the steady glow of
Christian manhood, and whose life-work had been
left unstained, either by schemes of selfishness or acts
of injustice. As the sun arose upon the busy world
the vast works, with their countless wheels, which
Thomas Dickson had set in motion and so long controlled, paused in respect to his memory; and it was
everywhere discovered that the MAN, lying so still in
the dignity of his rest, was indeed far greater than all
his works. He had simply passed through evening
shadows into a cloudless morning.

VIII.

" At evening time it shall be light."

CHRISTIAN BURIAL AND THE CHRISTIAN'S TOMB —
SHADOWS THE ASSURANCE OF LIGHT — CHAPLETS
FOR THE WORTHY MAN'S MONUMENT TEM-
PORAL AND UNFADING.

ON the second day of August, 1884, the remains
of Thomas Dickson were placed upon a special
train, which had been heavily draped and kindly
furnished for the use of the family and friends by
Samuel Sloan, the worthy President of the Delaware,
Lackawanna and Western Railway.   A whole train-
load of old friends from the valley, who had spon-
taneously gathered, accompanied the family with
their precious burden, under the leadership of Mr.
Dickson's confidential friend, Mr. Coe F. Young, and
his sons.   Citizens, business and professional men,

workmen, and friends in social life, from every walk and condition, pressed forward for the privilege of showing their affection for their departed associate and friend; and all along the way from Morristown to Scranton the deepest symbols of mourning testified of the hold that this man had taken on the heart of the people. The body was received with tearful silence by the citizens of Scranton and taken to the Dickson residence, where it remained in state for two days, in answer to the demand of the hundreds of workmen of all classes, who desired to look on the dead face of the man whom they had delighted to serve as a friend, while under his employment and official direction.

On the fourth day after his demise the funeral services took place from the family residence on Washington Avenue, conducted with befitting simplicity, according, as nearly as possible, with his well-known tastes, and desires often expressed. The services began at half-past one o'clock. Hundreds gathered to the funeral. Not only were the house and grounds filled to their utmost capacity, but the sidewalks and streets for a block or more away were packed with those who desired to pay the last tribute of their respect to this brother beloved. It had been announced at ten o'clock in the morning that those who desired could view the remains, and for more than two hours a constant stream of mourners passed through the gates of the Dickson mansion to

take a last look at his face. Hundreds of employees
of the Delaware and Hudson and of the Dickson
Manufacturing Companies were among this crowd;
and scores of men who had known him long years
ago, before he had achieved his life's work or had
made his great place in society. This procession
brought tender memories to his intimate friends of
those heart qualities that had so endeared him in the
years gone by, and as they passed from the doors not
a few of these workmen were seen wiping away the
tears of genuine grief.

At twelve o'clock the doors were closed and immediate preparations for the funeral were made; and
within half an hour the home was filled with the relatives and friends of the family. An especial train
arrived from New-York consisting of four heavily-
draped coaches, which brought a large party of ladies
and gentlemen from New York, and Morristown.
Many more had come from Honesdale, Carbondale,
Wilkesbarre, and Pittston, on special trains during
the morning. So that thousands of people had collected in silence when the time appointed for the
religious services had arrived. The casket was
placed in the front parlor of the mansion. On its lid
were laid palm leaves, the symbols of victory, with
a very few floral designs and mementos of family
affection. The funeral services were under the direction of his old friend and pastor, Rev. S. C. Logan,
D. D., of the First Presbyterian Church. The Rev.

Thomas R. Beeber, pastor of the Second Presbyterian Church of Scranton, opened the services with an appropriate prayer, which was filled with tenderest sympathy, wrought into beautiful sentences, and freighted with longings for the Comforter to sanctify this bereavement and sorrow to a whole community of mourners. The prayer closed with a petition for the bereaved household, characterized by singular sweetness. A quartet choir of the First Presbyterian Church, consisting of Mrs. Charles Watres, Miss Emily Platt, and Messrs. Horace E. and Wm. J. Hand, rendered the music with a tearful pathos.

The following account of these services is taken chiefly from the report made by the papers of that day, which was recognized as accurate at the time:

"After the reading of the Scriptures, Dr. Logan introduced Rev. Albert Erdman, D. D., pastor of the South Street Presbyterian Church at Morristown, N. J., who had ministered to Mr. Dickson in his last hours. Dr. Erdman's address was short, sympathetic, and elegant. It was especially appropriate by the testimony he gave of the religious faith manifested in the last hours of this business man. It brought lessons of wisdom and comfort to the great audience. He spoke in part as follows: 'It is my privilege to say a few words only of him for whom we all mourn, and toward whom we have so deep a regard — to refer briefly to him whose firm Christian character and whose traits of manhood so fully won for him the regard of all who knew him. It has been my privilege to know him only through the later years of his life; but it was my special privilege to be with him in the last week, which was so trying. It was my privilege to be with Mr. Dickson in his last hours, when he knew his days were numbered; and I stand here to bear to you living testimony of his Christian faith throughout his last sufferings. During his life he held responsible positions among his fellow-men — positions which involved care and constant, absolute attention. Yet, seemingly, he put these aside without effort, and reposed his whole trust in the Lord Jesus Christ. He manifested neither excitement nor alarm, but exhibited a staid trust in his Saviour, and in the belief that the everlasting arms would surround him when heart and flesh should fail. When the hour of trial came his blessed heritage of faith was a crowning glory of his useful life.

I am not here to pronounce a eulogy; and, remembering the character of the man, I know that such would not be his wish. His life is his best eulogy. But it is fit that this testimony of his trust should be given. His death was the beautiful ending of a noble life. It is hard to understand why a life so full of all that was good, so pure and free from that which could detract from its completeness, should be cut off so soon. But it is a grand solace to our hearts to know that Mr. Dickson was able to commit all things to his Redeemer. He has left the most precious heritage to his friends and to the world, by the conspicuous fidelity with which he has worked out a stewardship through an honorable and successful career.

"Dr. Logan then gave the funeral address, which was a beautiful tribute to Mr. Dickson's memory. This address was delivered without notes, and was apparently spontaneous. There was about it a pathos born of close friendship and intimacy in days gone by which could not be reproduced in print; and there were few who listened unmoved to this beautiful eulogy. Dr. Logan spoke as follows:

'If I could follow the feelings of my heart, I would sit down in silence to-day among the mourners of this smitten household; one with them in a sorrow which finds no true expression in words. To attempt to speak of the excellencies of Thomas Dickson seems to me much like attempting to publish my brother's virtues, which are the sacred home-treasures of hearts that knew how to love him. But as I look over this multitude, composed of all classes and callings of men, and remember how my friend took hold of the hearts of all who came in contact with him, I realize that we are but a very large family of mourners, gathered about the fallen tabernacle of him who was brother to us all. I am called upon simply to speak such words as we all would associate with our experience and remembrance of a useful and happy life.

'It strikes me as an exceedingly difficult thing to form, or express, a true and just summary of Mr. Dickson's characteristics and powers. God endowed him in his creation with such an excellent poise of faculties, and sent him on his pilgrimage of life with such a balance of powers, that to the great mass there was nothing striking or peculiar in him. Indeed, there was no excellency so striking to those who knew him best as this even poise of traits which constituted what we call his character. He always stood before us a quiet, full-orbed man, whose force we could readily feel and fully appreciate, but which we were never able intelligently to explain. He no doubt had weaknesses; but whatever weaknesses he had were so hidden away or neutralized by his natural endowments that they made little impression upon the world in which he moved. A weak side doubtless he had, but those who knew him never thought of seeking for it in their approaches. He was endowed with a clear and quick perception, which enabled him to reach his conclusions with a rapidity and clearness that seemed like intuition; and to announce his judgments with a completeness that seldom needed a revision. With a judgment never hasty, but ever controlled by a sense of justice which never seemed to be inactive in his soul; with a will inflexible to the purpose when once the end was clearly apprehended; a good natural persistence—and a wealth of resources seemingly inexhaustible; it is easy to see that he was born to be a leader of men. Yet, with it all, he had such qualities of heart that he never seemed to fail in his appreciation of men with whom he either came in contact or collision, in any of the various paths and responsibilities of his busy life. His social nature spread over all the ruggedness of his character, a glow of beauty, and filled him with a fountain of joy and fun that made him seem like a blood-brother to all kinds of men. The sunshine of his heart filled his pathway with scintillations of wit, and grotesque pictures of life, which gave both strength and elasticity to his steps, under the burden of duties; while his patience and persistence were sure, in the long run, to give him the victory.

'That which strikes us with the greatest force, perhaps, as we look over the long and varied life which has come to its earthly period, is the complete adaptation of our friend to the varied positions and circumstances he has occupied. Indeed, his endowments seem to have made him master of his circumstances. Whether we look at him when as a boy he struggled with adversity in the wilderness, having the care of a whole family on his young shoulders; or when, as a stripling, with the odds all against him, he searched for a path of successful life for himself, we find the same wealth of resources, the same perseverance and vivacity of spirit, which filled his labors with sunshine and song. As he arose step by step through the hard fields of enterprise, and occupied almost every station of labor and trust which a great company could give, he seemed to occupy each niche and position so completely that one might conclude he had been born to it.

'He showed himself both a leader of men and a master of the forces he was appointed to direct; whether as a workman in the shop, or as chief director in the chair of honor and responsibility. And what was stranger than all this was the fact that he seemed to be the same Thomas Dickson, whom men of all classes and callings were accustomed to call 'Tom,' in all stations and positions. His life was crowned with that healthfulness and honest success against which no man complained; and the expressions of his brain, and of his industry, are found in most of the grand enterprises which have made this whole valley historic. What his force was, as to its true measure, no man may say; but the silent power of his Christian charity and benevolence, as well as of his industry and full-rounded manhood, will be felt for many a day yet to come. His schemes were laid in truthfulness and justice, and conducted with honesty. Hence, their outwork and issues must bless and help mankind.

'How far such a life as this is shaped by the world, and how far its achievements are made successful through natural endowments, and how far determined by education, it is impossible perhaps for us to conclude. Mr. Dickson's education was found in the school of observation and experience. In an early life of poverty and struggle, he undoubtedly learned the great principles by which life can be made what God intended it to be. I love to think of him as the son of that old Scotch Presbyterian elder whose theory of education was housed in the single sentence, " Fear God and keep his commandments." I believe there was nothing in the life of this man more potent in determining its issues than the drill which he received from his parents in the sound doctrines embodied in the Westminster Catechism. His appreciation of humanity made him a friend of every man, and obtained for him the confidence of all workers, whether they were with him or under him. Hence the workmen were always his friends, and believed in him with unquestioning confidence.

' Illustrations of this confidence in him throughout this valley, with whose industries he has had so much to do, form an interesting part of its history. I give a single instance out of many which are familiar to us all, which will show something of the reality and extent of this confidence. Years ago the laborers in the upper part of the valley had settled upon the lands of the company of which Mr. Dickson was an employee, and were holding this land by irregular titles. This state of things had continued for years. At length difficulties arose, and lawyers on both sides were puzzling themselves under the cloud of two or three hundred lawsuits, when the laborers

took the matter in their own hands and came to the
Company with the proposition that if Thomas Dickson
would take hold of the matter, with full power to
act, they would abide by his decision without appeal
or complaint.   The proposition was accepted and the
settlement was made, and no complaint has been
heard from that day to this.

'What would seem in other men to be weaknesses,
under his sense of justice, charity, and good-nature
really had the force of virtues.   In discussing his
character the other night with a mutual friend who
knew him well, I was assured that his native stub-
bornness always seemed to win for himself friends,
and never made him permanent enemies.   Indeed,
I think he never lost a real friend.   Whatever position he occupied, he carried his associates in his heart,
and ever seemed to bear them with himself as he
outstripped them in the race of life.   The strains of
his favorite poet he loved to repeat, and we have all
heard it, again and again, as the very music of his
march in life:

"A man 's a man for a' that, and a' that."

The humblest of his associates will only learn by his
departure, how high above them his brains and his
energies raised him, and always held him.

'He was a man apparently without moods.   He
seemed never to change.   To us he was always the

same. Whether we met him in his office, overwhelmed with the burdens of business; on the highways of life and of leisure; or in the home of his rest and social enjoyments, he was always the same genial soul. There was no watching around office doors to find one's self in season to speak to the President of the Delaware and Hudson Company. He always seemed not only accessible, but actually waiting for the humblest man that had business with him.

'But it was in his Christian home that the best characteristics of our friend were manifested. Sustained by a wife and children who loved as well as honored him, he made his home an example which men of great schemes would do well to imitate. In his house was the church of the living God. It was a place where he could not only exercise his literary tastes, which were always urging him to another life than that which he lived; but where his rollicking, fun-loving nature found its fullest play, and filled every life about him with its sunshine. With his boundless Christian hospitality, he sanctified this house to hundreds of us who are gathered to-day to sympathize with its sorrow. Not a corner of it but is filled with mementos, to his wife and children, of his wit and his healthful home life.

'But we are here to bury our friend; and the place that knew him shall know him no more. We cannot believe that such a life, as this has been, is to pass into nothing. A poet has said, "An honest man is the noblest work of God," and we will not dispute it; but a Christian man, sanctified through the experiences and the duties of a faithful life, is a revelation as well as a work of God.   Indeed there is only one work of God that has ever surpassed it.   That is the revelation of the God-man who is the Saviour of men.   The faithful Christian, in the lower sense, is "the Word made flesh," to dwell and walk among men ; and every sanctified human life is a power, under the Divine administration, for the elevation and purification of the race.   God will see to it that such a life as this, which has passed from sight, shall sweep forward with its living potency until the very end shall come.   The world will always be the better for Thomas Dickson's having lived in it.

'I once stood in a valley of the Alps and watched the setting of the sun at the close of a beautiful day. Inch by inch the light crept up the mountain side, as the day died down in the valley.   Long after the deepest shadows had fallen where I stood, I saw the golden sunlight gilding the peaks with its glory. There it hung after night had begun, in the valley; not only a memento of the day that was already dead, but a prophesy and harbinger of a new day that was to come.   So it strikes me now as I stand by this fallen brother.   Such a life as this has its high sunshine as well as its night; and as we stand at the meeting-point of the past and future, it gives us the fullest assurance of the coming day, as well as

the precious remembrance of the day that has closed
and gone.

> " So, when a good man dies,
> For years beyond our ken
> The light he leaves behind him lies
> Upon the paths of men."

'Business men, and brothers! gathered here to-
day; burdened with great schemes, and surrounded
with innumerable temptations, you must know that
you, too, shall soon pass away. The places and paths
that know you now shall soon know you no more.
Let me ask you, with a brother's earnestness, to seek
for that anchorage of life which is only found by a
living faith in an ever-living Redeemer. It was the
permanent peace and sublime potency wrought by
this faith which made the life of Thomas Dickson
blessed and happy through his three-score years;
as well as successful in the stewardship which God
gave him. It was this faith which made his death so
peaceful and sublime. Every man should make a
true estimate of himself, first of all, in laying out the
business of his life; and that estimate will be found
more than defective which makes no certain provision
for death, and the eternity of the soul. Our own
Christian poet has said:

> " Lives of great men all remind us
> We can make our lives sublime,
> And, departing, leave behind us
> Foot-prints on the sands of time."

9

' But God has told us that he who builds on this Gospel foundation which He has laid—this foundation of a Christian faith—"shall never be moved." Though such a man shall die, our Lord has said, " YET SHALL HE LIVE."

'All the comfort that we can give this household, in our deepest sympathy, can amount to very little ; but God can comfort them ; and comfort us, as we go from this house of mourning to complete our pilgrimage of life. Let us, then, commend them and ourselves to this grace which can never fail.'

"Dr. Logan closed his address with an earnest prayer for the comfort of the family, and the choir sang the sacred hymn, 'Jesus, lover of my soul.'"

The body was then borne away by the associates and co-workers of the dead brother and friend to the house appointed for all the living.

These business associates and friends were: Messrs. A. H. Vandling, J. E. Chittenden, E. W. Weston, C. D. Hamond, T. H. Voorhees, and Rolin Manville, all of whom were connected with the Delaware and Hudson Canal Company. His honorable pall-bearers were Hugh J. Jewett, President of the Erie Railway, F. S. Winston, President of the Mutual Life Insurance Company, J. R. Taylor and W. H. Tillinghast, of the Reading Railroad, Benjamin G. Clark, of the Lackawanna Iron and Coal Co., Samuel Sloan, President of the Delaware, Lackawanna and Western

Railroad, Le Grand B. Cannon, of the Delaware and Hudson, G. De B. Keim, of the Philadelphia and Reading, David Dows, of the Delaware and Hudson, and E. P. Wilbur, of the Lehigh Valley Railways. These honored and worthy gentlemen walked beside the hearse with silent meditation, as real mourners of a fallen brother.

The procession wound its way to the Dunmore cemetery between rows of the silent workmen and their families, who stood with uncovered heads, filling both sides of the street for a full mile and a half; and many a silent tear told of the more than mere respect for the dead which had gathered the working-people to witness these funeral solemnities.

The remains were conveyed to their last resting-place while clouds hung low and threatening; and the heavy-hearted multitude returned to the city with silent lips. But as the mourners left the cemetery the mists rolled back, and the sun burst from behind the clouds; and a beautiful rainbow arched its prismatic colors above the new-made grave, which seemed but an emblem and an omen of the beautiful memory left by the brilliant achievements, and the unblemished purity, that had marked the life, and illustrated the career, of Thomas Dickson.

The bereaved widow and her afflicted children had hardly gathered, in their sympathy of sorrow, in the deserted homestead, which had preserved so

many precious remembrances of the departed father
and husband, when Testimonials from the outside
world began to come to them, filled with sincere and
graceful assurances of appreciation of the excellence
of a departed friend, and of touching sympathy with
his sorrowing family.   These testimonials came from
churches, societies, and business corporations with
which Mr. Dickson had been associated, and were
freighted with honest and tender estimates of his
character and work.   Many of these testimonials
were executed in the richest style of art, and contained
exquisite manifestations of taste.   His associates in
business and in Christian work chiseled, by these
parchment rolls, and tastefully-mounted books of
affectionate testimonial, the graceful monument for
Thomas Dickson's grave; and thus wove unfading
chaplets for his memory.   Their greatest excellence
is found in the fact that their truth, and appro-
priateness, could not be questioned by any who
knew him.

I deem it entirely appropriate to close this brief
record of a worthy life; this memorial of my excellent friend, with a few of these testimonials, which
may be accepted as specimens of the whole, and
taken as the expression of the thought and honest
heart-appreciation of that whole world in which he
wrought; and with which he lived and died in such
beautiful and profound sympathy.   No attempt is
made to reproduce the beautiful forms in which these

testimonials were presented. They will be kept as precious heir-looms by children's children.

They are as follows:

I.

THE DICKSON MANUFACTURING COMPANY.

Extract from the Minutes of a meeting of Directors and Stockholders of the Dickson Manufacturing Company, held in Scranton, Pa., August 1st, 1884.

THE Directors and Stockholders of this Company have learned with great sorrow of the death of our associate and friend,

THOMAS DICKSON,

and we desire to indicate upon the minutes of this Corporation the following estimate of his character and expression of our loss.

THOMAS DICKSON was a man of strong native talent, elevated tastes, great executive power, firm in his convictions and principles; a man of STERLING HONESTY, singleness of purpose, broad in his conceptions, and possessed of high courage and indomitable will. As a man of business he was courteous in his intercourse with all men; successful in all his enterprises; and possessed of that frugality, and energy, which inspired all who were associated with him with HOPE AND CONFIDENCE.

As a member of this community we testify to his public spirit, his generosity and strong friendship, which have endeared him to all who have come in contact with him, both as employees and as associate directors; and have given him a popularity in all this community that is the sure indication OF HIGH WORTH.

His contributions to and sympathy with all philanthropic enterprises were constant and well timed.

In all our intercourse with him we have found him a man of the strictest integrity, and true to his Christian faith and profession. His warmest friends are found as well among the poor as the rich. Tears fall easily at his bier. The growth of this Company, founded by him, and the great business and material growth of Lackawanna Valley; and of large corporate enterprises beyond this State, present a worthy monument of his character and work. His high success from humble beginnings against difficulties and obstacles are an honor to our AMERICAN INSTITUTIONS, showing that energy, merit, and true ambition will meet their reward.

We mourn the loss of such an associate and friend.

We sympathize most deeply with the partner of his life and with his family in this their sorrow.

J. C. PLATT,
    Secretary.

GEORGE L. DICKSON,
    Chairman.

II.

THE FIRST NATIONAL BANK OF SCRANTON.

AT a meeting of the Directors of the First National Bank of Scranton, held August 4th, it was deemed due to the memory of THOMAS DICKSON, who departed this life on the evening of July 31st, 1884, to adopt and place upon record the following minute:

THOMAS DICKSON was one of the original corporators of this bank, and, up to the time of his death, one of its most honored and trusted directors.

His conservative views and his wise foresight have, in all our intercourse with him, impressed upon us the conviction that he was ever a wise counselor and strong executive officer.

His deep interest in this institution, and his cöoperation in all measures in its behalf, will ever be a pleasant recollection to us.

His constant success in all undertakings, and his unbounded integrity, have brought to us that hope and confidence which is the life and support of business.

In times of financial depression his wisdom and courage never failed; in times of prosperity he was never carried beyond the line of prudence and safety.

We feel deeply the loss of his presence in our councils.

The influence of a man of such strength, as he possessed, will long be felt in the business interests of this community. It is through such men that institutions are made stable.

We bear to his afflicted family our deepest sympathy in their trials; and direct that a copy of this minute, signed by the President, and attested by the secretary, be presented to them.

Attest: J. A. LINEN,   JOSEPH J. ALBRIGHT,
            Secretary.   *President.*

III.

THE MOOSIC POWDER COMPANY.

A T a special meeting of the Directors of the Moosic Powder Company at their office in Scranton, Pa., at 8 o'clock, P. M., August 4th, 1884, to take action commemorative of the death of THOMAS DICKSON, one of the founders of the Company; for many years an active director in its management; and always its earnest friend and wise counselor, H. S. Pierce was made Chairman and E. W. Weston Secretary.

It was Resolved, That, while bowing in submission and sorrow to that dispensation of an overruling and all-wise Providence, which removed from us by death, on the evening of July 31st, 1884, our friend and associate, THOMAS DICKSON; we, as a body, desire hereby to place on record our high appreciation and esteem of him as an associate, and a man, and our grief at his loss; and to bear tribute to his memory, which shall ever be cherished by us, and held dear and sacred.

Thomas Dickson was a man whom to know was to love; with whom to be associated was to honor and respect; a man of noble and generous impulses, whose aim was ever to promote the welfare and happiness of his fellow-men; always ready to lend a listening ear, to give a helping hand, an encouraging word, and a sympathizing heart, to the worthy.

He was a man, foremost in every good work, "given to hospitality," "diligent in business, fervent in spirit, serving the Lord." Of quick perception, of remarkable clearness and grasp of mind; of sound and unbiased judgment; he was always a trustworthy friend and adviser. A man of high social qualifications and attainments, courteous, unselfish, and affable in his nature and in all intercourse with those with whom he was brought in contact; of strict integrity, honorable, and above suspicion in all his dealings. Firm and decided in his convictions; confident and courageous in his undertakings; he was fearless and unhesitating in the discharge of every duty.

We mourn his loss to us, to this community, and to the world, as creating a void that cannot be filled.

To his bereaved wife and afflicted family we give assurance of our heartfelt sympathy in this dark hour of grief and sorrow, and pray that Heaven's choicest blessings may rest upon and attend them.

A copy of this resolution shall be presented to the family and entered on the minutes.

E. W. WESTON,
Secretary.

H. S. PIERCE,
Chairman.

IV.

THE CROWN POINT IRON COMPANY.

AT a meeting of the Board of Directors of the Crown Point Iron Company, held at their office in New York Nov. 25th, 1884, the following was ordered placed upon the minutes:

It is with the deepest sorrow that we record upon our minutes the death of our friend and co-Director, THOMAS DICKSON, Esq. He was one of the corporators of this Company, and was ever most warmly interested in its success.

Faithful in the discharge of every duty, and guided by a sound judgment, we mourn his death as an honored friend, as well as a valued adviser.

His memory will be cherished by us with deep regret for his departure, and ever-affectionate regard; and we desire to extend to his family the warmest expression of our sympathy in their great bereavement.

L. G. B. CANNON,
President.

NEW-YORK, Dec. 8th, 1884.

V.

DELAWARE AND HUDSON CANAL COMPANY.

AT a special meeting of the Board of Managers of the Delaware and Hudson Canal Company, held at the office of the Company on Saturday, August 2d, 1884, to take action in regard to the death of their late president, Mr. THOMAS DICKSON, the following preamble and resolutions were adopted:

With unfeigned sorrow the Board of Managers of the Delaware and Hudson Canal Company record upon their minutes the following tribute of their respect for the memory of their friend and associate,

THOMAS DICKSON,

who departed this life on the 31st of July, 1884.

He was born in the year when action was taken for the formation of this Company, and he was in its service from his youth.

He became its Superintendent in 1860; in 1867 he was appointed Vice-President; in 1869 he was elected President, and filled that office until the time of his death. His life was thus identified with the Company's progress. With every detail in its working that life was wrought out, and it unfolded with every step in its development. His advancement was in its prosperity, and its reverses came home to him with perhaps more of nearness than any personal loss. Such unity of interest with the institution to whose service he was devoted marked him out as the man to whom the highest office in its gift would necessarily fall.

Being invested with it, he adorned his Presidency by bringing to bear upon its duties the whole weight of a rare condition of mental and moral endowments. With all the cordiality and loyalty of his nature, he carried out the broad policy of development which had marked the administration of his predecessor in the office, and with which he had always been in generous sympathy. To insure the success of his noble work, he was furnished with an intellectual strength, a faculty of rapid and accurate judgment, a power to grasp and arrange multifarious details, and an intuitive knowledge of men, which, together with his immense power of will, communicated a unity and a momentum to his endeavors that compelled universal respect.

In the discharge of his official duties he showed a calm reserve and a clearly-defined high purpose of well-doing, which betokened the real greatness of his character; while in his personal relations, as their chief, with his fellow-servants of the Company of every grade, he won their admiration by the quiet amenity and noble consistency of his life.

Perhaps no exhibition of his great power to influence others was more marked—certainly none was more honorable—than that which was brought out on occasions of controversy with other Companies. In the composition of these his breadth of view in suggestions of policy, his judicial moderation in presenting the claims which he represented, and his manifest anxiety to reconcile the interests of all, upon a foundation of justice to all, led many, who have admired his course, to regard him as the peacemaker among his fellows; and in the limited time since his death more than one of these companies have referred to this trait of his character. But in all the relations of life, private as well as official, he was the same highly-esteemed, respected, honored, and beloved man. And while, in the expression of our sorrow, we spread upon these records our testimonial of regard for our departed friend, we are reminded of the weightier burden of grief of those whose relations of love and kindred bring home to them a greater poignancy of suffering. Be it therefore

Resolved, I. That the Board of Managers of this Company tender to the family of Mr. DICKSON the assurance of their deepest sympathy in a bereavement which will be felt far beyond the limits of the home where he was so tenderly beloved.

Resolved, II. That this Board will attend the funeral of Mr. DICKSON on the 4th inst., and will direct the various offices of the Company to be closed on that day.

Resolved, III. That the foregoing minute be adopted and spread upon the records, and that an engrossed copy thereof be transmitted to the family of Mr. DICKSON.

F. M. OLYPHANT,
Secretary.

VI.

MUTUAL LIFE INSURANCE COMPANY.

AT a special meeting of the Board of Trustees of The Mutual Life Insurance Company of New York, held August 1st, 1884, the president addressed the Board as follows:

Gentlemen: I announce, with sincere regret, the death of another Trustee of this Company —

THOMAS DICKSON.

He died at Morristown, N. J., last evening, July 31st, of disease of the heart.

He was born in Berwickshire, Scotland, and at his death was sixty years of age.

Mr. DICKSON was elected a Trustee of this Company November 19th, 1873, and has served, most intelligently and acceptably, as a member of the committees on Insurance Agencies, Mortuary Claims, and Nominations. Each of these committees will miss his dignified and courteous presence, his practical knowledge and sound judgment, in their deliberations and acts. The executive officers will miss his kind interest, and wise counsels, in the affairs of the Company; and not less his personal sympathy and friendship. Other members of the Board, who have been associated with him, here and elsewhere, and knew and appreciated his sterling character and worth, will now address you; and will furnish a more fitting testimonial of the appreciation of this Board for our late Trustee, and their sincere sympathy for his family in their great affliction.

Hon. John E. Develin said:

Mr. President: The heavy affliction which has fallen upon us almost deprives me of the ability to speak in regard to it. Mr. Dickson rose from the ranks by a wonderful mental power — a gift from above. By great industry, integrity, and honesty, he elevated himself to one of the most prominent and influential positions in the country. After he became a member of this Board, his activity, his attention to its affairs, and his conscientious discharge of his duty were marked by all his associates.

His loss to the Company is a great one.

Mr. SEWELL read the following resolutions and moved their adoption :

Whereas, It has pleased Almighty God in his Providence to remove from his earthly sphere our late fellow-member of this Board of Trustees,

THOMAS DICKSON,

Be it Resolved, That this Board have heard the sad intelligence with deep regret, and that we avail ourselves of the earliest opportunity to make an expression of our sorrow.

Our deceased friend was a man of ripe experience, sound judgment, positive convictions, and decisive will, while his honesty and integrity were above the shadow of suspicion. In every position where his good sense, business experience, and unquestioned integrity, had placed him (and these qualities made him sought after by many), he discharged the duties intrusted to him with diligence, prudence, careful attention to all the necessary details, and a sagacity which was the result of his training and his long identification with large business interests. Whether as the executive head of a great Railroad, Canal and Coal Company, a Trustee of this Corporation, or a simple citizen of the Republic, he was ever solicitous to discharge his duties with zeal, intelligence, and a conscientious regard for the rights of all persons who might in any way be interested in the trusts over which he was called upon to preside. In this Board, as a member of it, and of several of its important committees, his loss will be deeply felt, and is feelingly deplored. But while we sorrow over his bier we permit ourselves to take pardonable pride in the record of his pure life, of his duties fulfilled, and of his work completed; while we sincerely desire to join with our deceased brother in the good hope which he enjoyed of a glorious immortality.

Resolved, That these resolutions be inscribed on the minutes, and copies thereof be sent to the family of the deceased gentleman.

This motion was seconded by Mr. George S. Coe, by Mr. Julian T. Davies, and by Mr. Frederic Cromwell.

Mr. Coe said:

Mr. Chairman: The circumstances of this day remind me very strongly of the position in which we all stand. Mr. Dickson was a member of the Committee on Mortuary Claims, of which I am also a member. The duties of that committee vividly bring before us the fact that we stand, as it were, upon the confines of two worlds. If we are not reminded by our official duties in connection with that committee of our own mortality, we are certainly impressed by the dropping away of our associates in such numbers. Mr. Dickson, as a member of this · committee, was very attentive, very kind, and everything he did was always most acceptable. He discharged his duties with great intelligence and great wisdom, and we most sincerely regret to lose him. I can only add that I heartily concur in everything that has been said, and I join all the members here in sincere regret at his death.

Mr. Davies said:

Mr. President: I had not an intimate acquaintance with Mr. Dickson, but I had marked his presence at this Board. The intercourse that I had with him in connection with the performance of duties, as Trustees of this Company, was principally in the examination of the securities of the Company. I remember being very much struck by the care, and accuracy, he displayed, and the fidelity with which this gentleman, who presided over public enterprises of vast importance; who was President of one of the greatest companies connected with the coal interest of this country; and whose private interests were so large, attended, day after day, and hour after hour, with his own hands counting securities; examining their denominations, and going through all the minute details of a careful, personal examination of the assets of this Company. And it seemed to me as if, in the care with which he performed the details of these duties, was to be found the secret of Mr. Dickson's success in life. Every duty, doubtless, that came to his hand, whether great or small, was performed with equal fidelity. In manner he was courteous and considerate. For all of us he had a pleasant greeting; and even a slight acquaintance with him could not fail to leave upon the mind a pleasant and enduring impression. We have lost from this Board one of its most valued members; a man whose place it will be very hard to fill.

Among the gravest acts that fall upon this body, and upon the more experienced members of it, is the filling of the places of these really great men who have passed away. Certainly, one of the greatest minds that I have known in this Board left us on the death of Mr. Dickson.

Mr. Olyphant said:

Mr. President and Gentlemen: It seems hardly necessary to say more than has been said; but I have known Mr. Dickson as a friend from my early boyhood, and my feelings prompt me to add a few words. A good man has passed away. Wherever Mr. Dickson's lot was cast he had the respect of the community around him, while those who were allowed to come into the nearer relations of friendship, came to love as well as to respect him. His calm yet vigor-

ous intellect was given with untiring devotion to the
company over which he presided ; yet we know here
how unselfishly he gave his time, and the remains of
strength, to help forward the prosperity of this great
corporation.   Whatever he did he desired to do well ;
for his estimate of duty was very exacting.   His last
sickness came upon him suddenly. Rest was needed,
but the man hitherto strong and active could not be
convinced of this necessity.   He pressed on, prefer-
ring, as it seemed, to die in harness rather than to
rust out.   In his home, surrounded by all that was
attractive, and deeply mourned as husband, father,
brother, friend, he passed away.   We cannot lift the
veil from the mystery of such a Providence.   We
must leave it where our friend left it, and trust that
when our time comes to follow him we may be able
to say, and feel, as he said, just before he passed
away—his last words—" It is all right."

The resolutions were thereupon adopted.

On motion of Mr. Develin, the President was au-
thorized to select a delegation to attend the funeral,
at Scranton, on Monday, the 4th instant.

Mr. Andrews, who was in Canada when he heard
of Mr. Dickson's death, telegraphed the following as
his tribute to the memory of the deceased :

Mr. Dickson's mental qualities were singularly well
poised.   Possessing ability of the highest order, it

was sweetly tempered by modesty. Quick in reaching conclusions, he was never rash. A rigid disciplinarian, he avoided harshness in reproof. Earnest in expression, he was considerate of the feelings of those from whom he differed. Deeply religious, he shunned the appearance of austerity. Trained in a school where self-assertion was a merit, he never lost the quality of diffidence. Indeed, in all the attributes of his mind he approached in a marvelous degree to the ideal of that rarest of characters—

A CHRISTIAN GENTLEMAN.

At a subsequent meeting of the Board of Trustees the President made the following report, viz.:

To fulfill the duty you laid upon me, to aid in paying the last rites of sympathy and respect to our late associate and friend Thomas Dickson, I attended his funeral at the city of Scranton, with Mr. Holden, Mr. Olyphant, and Mr. Henderson of our Board of Trustees, on Monday, August 4th. The family residence was filled with Mr. Dickson's personal friends and neighbors, while a much larger number of them, who could not find room, remained at the entrance and in the streets near the house until the services were ended.

The cemetery was two miles distant. As the long funeral procession wound its way through the valleys, over the hills, and past the open shafts leading to the mines beneath them, the busy scenes of our friend's early life and labors, and of his subsequent history, were spread out before us.   On the roadside, at short intervals, stood large crowds of men, women, and children, from the various workshops and mines, with uncovered heads, watching with sad, sympathetic eyes, the remains of their cherished friend passing to their last resting-place.   No funeral pomp or studied eulogy could so eloquently, and touchingly assure us of the place he filled in the hearts and minds of the people, as the mute sorrow expressed in every coun- tenance; as the multitude watched this procession on its way to bury their friend out of their sight.   From the entrance at the cemetery to the open grave, the path, and the ground around it were covered with evergreens and flowers, on which his chosen friends, who had borne his body to its last earthly home, placed the coffin.   Then, as they reverently depos- ited the body in its narrow resting-place, they sung with sweet melody these touching words:

> " Unveil thy bosom, faithful tomb,
>   Take this new treasure to thy trust;
> And give these sacred relics room
>   To seek a slumber in the dust.
>
> Nor pain, nor grief, nor anxious fear
>   Invade thy bounds — no mortal woes
> Can reach the peaceful sleeper here,
>   While angels watch the soft repose.

So Jesus slept — God's dying Son
    Pass'd thro' the grave and blest the bed :
Rest here, blest saint, till from his throne
    The morning breaks to pierce the shades.

Break from his throne, illustrious morn :
    Attend, O Earth ! his sovereign word ;
Restore thy trust — a glorious form
    Called to ascend and meet the Lord."

And so we committed his body to the ground, "earth to earth, ashes to ashes, dust to dust," in full hope of that day when this body shall be changed and made like to "His glorious body," who burst the bonds of death, and brought "life and immortality to light," for all those who believe in Him.

It seems strange to us to see a man of wisdom and strength, of purity and power, while intently and with his whole heart fulfilling, to the utmost, his wide and weighty duties to his God, and his fellow-man, thus stricken down in the meridian of his life and labors; with so much to do, and so much undone. So he once thought, till he received his death-bed lesson of filial trust in his Heavenly Father; then he had faith to exclaim, in these his last words while in the agonies of dissolution, "IT IS ALL RIGHT," and thus passed to his eternal rest.

An extract from the minutes.

(Signed)   RICHARD A. McCURDY,
Vice-President and Ex-Officio Secretary to the Board.

CLOSING WORDS.

THE mystery of human life is never more impress-
ive than when we pause to consider the void,
and the adjustment of forces, which its earthly completion has demanded. There is, first, a solemn halt
in the tread of toil, when a great worker falls, then a
walking softly for a time, as if the listeners had learned
the cause of the shock, and then follows a passing on
in solemn meditation to complete the work required.
There is hardly visible the turning of a hair's breadth
in the trend of the world's life, or in the march of men,
by the fall of the greatest of men. The business world
moves on as if little dependent upon the individuals
that determine its control ; and we wonder at it. But
there can, perhaps, be no more forceful testimony
given to the completeness of the earthly life, or the
faithfulness of the stewardship, of any marked worker

in business schemes than the leaving of all trusts without shock or derangement. The levers and pulleys, the cogs and springs, of the great machine must have been both accurately and wisely adjusted, if they run on, without friction, after the master-hand that invented, and ever controlled, them has been suddenly removed. Such is the testimony which was given to the completeness of the earthly stewardship of THOMAS DICKSON. The diameters of his power, and the circles of his varied influence were so wide, and decided, that the business world wondered what might be the result of the surrender of his trusts and of his departure from the world. But it was found that the master-mind had so wisely adjusted his machinery, and balanced his industries, and had so faithfully wrought out his designs, that little remained unfinished. His offices and his beautiful homes were left as types of his life, as well as of his completed task. From foundation to cap-stone every part was in its place; all things finished and furnished to their ends; henceforth subject simply to the wear and tear of time. His chapter in the world's life and history, whether adjudged long or short, great or small, was completed; and henceforth must stand, in the memory of his associates, in its striking symmetry and manifold excellence.

So complete was his life that the social circle of which he was the center, and the household of which he was the life, moved on along the lines of his appointment, hardly realizing his departure. His quiet, masterly spirit, his modest gentleness of dignity, his genial sunshine and sparkling humor, lingered so vividly in all the paths of his work, and his resting, that his wife, his children, and his intimate friends walked on as if still in his company, ever and anon to be startled with the fact that comes with its benumbing force to assure them that he has entirely outstripped them, and now walks in a sphere higher than human vision can reach. He has passed through and beyond the shadows to the cloudless morning, leaving the last echo of his voice, "It is all right," to cheer and strengthen our faith with the signal as from the other shore.

But he has also left the marks of his genius, and character, in all the paths of his pilgrimage ; deeply carved on all his great and beneficent works ; and with these would he draw us onward, and ever upward, to the gladness of the coming meeting.

For the purpose, if possible, of deepening these marks, and clearing them of the mosses that time weaves to cover and deface them — after the manner of Old Mortality, who chiseled anew the tomb inscriptions of the Scotch Martyrs — has this Tablet been written. In the awkward scratches and manifest imperfections may be readily discerned the inexpert and uncertain hand of the artist; but these must be ignored by all who would see the excellence, and feel the force, of the original inscriptions. Whatever

may be the defects that mar the tablet, they can hardly obscure, if they do not actually reveal, the sincerity and affectionate aim of the rude chisel. This whole Household Tablet has been wrought under the solemn conviction that such a many-sided man — such a husband, father, and friend — deserves to be held in perpetual remembrance. May the shadow of his excellence ever fall upon his children's children as the benediction of the blessed.

www.ingramcontent.com/pod-product-compliance
Lightning Source LLC
Chambersburg PA
CBHW020229030726
47497CB00009B/3008